NINE LADIES DANCING

NINE LADIES DANCING

DEBORAH M. HATHAWAY

BOOKS BY DEBORAH M. HATHAWAY

Stand Alone Novels

A Secret Fire

When Two Rivers Meet

To Warm a Wintered Heart

A Cornish Romance Series

On the Shores of Tregalwen, a Novella

Behind the Light of Golowduyn, Book One

For the Lady of Lowena, Book Two

Near the Ruins of Penharrow, Book Three

Belles of Christmas Multi-Author Series

Nine Ladies Dancing, Book Four

Belles of Christmas - Frost Fair
Multi-Author Series

On the Second Day of Christmas, Book Four

*For all those who love Christmas
as much as I do.*

*There's nothing quite like
the magic, the love, and the hope
this time of year brings.*

Belles of Christmas

Book 1 - Unmasking Lady Caroline by Mindy Burbidge Strunk
Book 2 - Goodwill for the Gentleman by Martha Keyes
Book 3 - The Earl's Mistletoe Match by Ashtyn Newbold
Book 4 - Nine Ladies Dancing by Deborah M. Hathaway
Book 5 - A Duke for Lady Eve by Kasey Stockton

Belles of Christmas - Frost Fair

Book 1 – Her Silent Knight by Ashtyn Newbold
Book 2 – All is Mary and Bright by Kasey Stockton
Book 3 – Thawing the Viscount's Heart by Mindy Burbidge Strunk
Book 4 – On the Second Day of Christmas by Deborah M. Hathaway
Book 5 – The Christmas Foundling by Martha Keyes

These books may be read in any order.

CHAPTER 1

ondon, December

Crystal chandeliers, adorned with hundreds of candles, hung from vaulted ceilings, brightening the vast ballroom. By the warmth pervading the townhome, one would never guess the sun had already set, causing the frigid, December air to permeate through all of London.

Despite the bitter cold raging outside, and the heat swirling round the masqueraders, Meg Baker had never felt more at ease. She stood in a cool, darkened corridor, tucked in the corner of the grand room. Out of sight from the dancers, parents, and gossipers alike, she tapped her foot in time with the music.

From her secluded vantage point, her eyes trailed around the stunning elegance of the ballroom. White, delicate carvings of flowers and vines trimmed the towering, light blue walls, like frost at the edge of a frozen lake. The candles' light twirled across the wooden flooring, the bright glow following the men and women as they danced with one another in their elaborate costumes.

The image was a spectacle, indeed. A sight no one could help but admire. A sight everyone wished to be surrounded by. Everyone, that is, but Meg. Of course, any other evening she would have been

1

one of the primary dancers, more than happy to take part in all the excitement until the sun rose again over the frozen Thames.

But that night, she was far too distracted by a certain gentleman standing with her in the corridor to wish to be anywhere else but with him.

"Should we really be hiding away in here, Matthew?" she asked in a hushed tone. "Are we not to dance, like the rest of the guests?"

"I will not stop you," Matthew replied. "If you wish to leave, you are welcome to. I know how you love to dance." He paused, taking on the appearance of a faultless victim—rounded eyes, lowered lips, eyebrows together. "I'll be fine on my own. Merely…lonely."

She propped a hand on her hip and shook her head half-heartedly. "You haven't changed a bit, have you? You are still the same tease you have always been."

In an instant, his sorrowful expression lifted to one of mirth. "And I always will be." He winked, sending her heart into a flapping frenzy.

No, Matthew had not changed.

But Meg's feelings for him *had*.

In the dim light of the corridor, she studied him. His light brown hair was tousled as usual, as if he'd just come in from a brisk ride on his gelding. She could barely see the hazel in his eyes, due to the simple black and white mask covering the upper portion of his face.

Those eyes had always held a mischievous glint. Meg had noticed that straightaway when she'd first met him as a nine-year-old. Matthew and his twin sister Louisa were twelve when Matthew's father inherited Hollridge House—a neighboring estate —from a distant cousin.

She and the twins were inseparable, spending every moment they could together, up until Matthew had left for university. While he studied and schooled, Meg had courted, danced, and flirted with any gentleman she wished. But no one, she quickly discovered, could compare to Matthew.

"Why are you staring at me like that?"

Meg blinked, her cheeks burning as she realized she'd been gaping. "I was merely considering your costume. That is all."

He leaned against the side of the wall, crossing his feet in front of him as he folded his arms. "You take issue with it?"

She scaled him head to toe. He'd always been much taller than she was by nearly a foot, but since starting school, his shoulders had filled in, and his jaw had squared. She'd forever considered him handsome, but now…now her pulse raced.

His costume. Right. They were speaking of his costume. She eyed his simple black jacket, breeches, and shoes. "I would hardly consider what you are wearing a costume."

"I shall have you know, I worked very hard on this."

"But it is just a mask."

"A mask that took hours to find. I had to borrow this one from a friend. But if you are disappointed in my efforts, you must hold my parents responsible. They didn't tell me we were attending the masquerade until after they retrieved me from Oxford yesterday."

"Of course."

Meg had been invited to join the Pratts on a short visit to London while Mr. and Mrs. Pratt brought Matthew back from Oxford. Meg's parents were away with friends in Scotland for the winter months, as per their tradition, so Meg could either go with the Pratts or remain at home alone. As she had not seen Matthew since October, her decision had been easily made.

"So you see?" Matthew continued. "I have had very little time to prepare a costume at all."

"Yes," she said, "but what are you supposed to be? A mole?"

"A badger, Miss Baker. A *badger*." He did a flourishing gesture of his hands across his black and white mask. "Clearly."

"Very well, but that does not explain the green of your waistcoat. I don't recall many badgers having olive-colored stomachs."

He stared down at his chest. "It's but a small grass stain. One tends to pick them up when one crawls around on four little legs."

Her laughter echoed down the dark corridor behind them. Matthew's warning scowl contrasted with his shining eyes.

"Hush," he chided. "I do not wish to be discovered. You may not mind dancing, but I do. Especially with insects."

She followed his eyes past a family of seven dressed as swans to where a lady attired in a bee costume hummed past them. "You very well could be stung by some of the women out there," she said. "But you must know that a *deer* would never harm you."

"Especially not one as lovely as you."

She glowed. Her costume had taken ages to create. She did not think transforming into a doe would be so very difficult, but brown was not the most flattering of colors. Instead, she'd opted for a simple white dress to represent the white of the doe's belly, and a short, reddish brown fur cape that draped down her back. Her tan mask hid her identity well, and though the black nose did not protrude far from her face, the long, rounded ears on her headpiece perfectly revealed what animal she portrayed.

Compliments had abounded for her earlier in the evening, but they were all forgotten as Matthew's words warmed her through.

"Then perhaps you would not mind dancing again with said deer," she said, rounding her eyes innocently, much like a doe's. "After all, you know your mother would be upset if she found you in here, hiding away at yet another party."

She gave him a knowing look. It was no secret that Mrs. Pratt didn't approve of her son's desire to avoid Society and responsibility. She wanted him to stop attending school and to make more of an effort to help his father with matters of the estate Matthew was to inherit. Matthew, however, was not one for change, or socializing. Meg knew he'd always far preferred a quiet, simple life. One without pressure from his mother and an estate.

He shrugged. "It is fortunate we have chosen such a secluded location then. She will not find us in here, nor will anyone else for that matter. And as for your suggestion to dance, we wouldn't wish for the gossips to start on us already. Two dances in one evening would surely get them to talk."

Meg's smile faltered. Was he truly worried over the potential gossip, or did he simply not wish to dance with her?

"Perhaps we may find you another amiable partner?" He moved

4

closer to the entryway of the corridor and the ballroom, peering at the dancers. "What about the gentleman in the tawny owl costume? Your colors would certainly match with his."

Meg eyed the man's movements as he weaved in and out of the set of dancers in his brown, feathered regalia, as graceful as any bird. "We *would* match. However, he dances so fine, I fear I would appear more as a newborn fawn than as an elegant doe."

Matthew chuckled, his throat bobbing up and down—a sight only visible due to his poorly tied cravat. He'd always been too humble to care much about his image. Meg loved that about him.

"Very well. No owl. What about the wolf in the black mask?"

Meg narrowed her eyes. "I believe that is the Duke of Alverton. I did not know he was in attendance this evening. An amiable partner, I daresay. But, oh, do you see how his eyes remain on his partner, the fox with the jeweled mask? He's clearly taken with her. No, I would never do for him."

She was clearly creating these issues merely to avoid dancing with any other gentleman, but Matthew hardly seemed aware as he scratched his jaw. "It would appear that choosing a partner for you is not as easy as I thought." His eyes moved over the crowds. "Well, what of the squirrel dancing with my sister? If he is good enough for Louisa, he ought to be good enough for you, yes?"

Meg followed his pointed finger to where Louisa Pratt danced in her fish costume. Colorful ribbons weaved in and out of her hair in loops resembling scales, and her mask covered most of her face in the same colorful pattern. She danced with a man whose orange, fur-covered shoulders stretched wide.

"Oh, dear. Mr. Abbott. I was hoping her costume would have prevented him from finding her again."

Matthew raised a brow barely visible above his small mask. She leaned closer to him, a hint of his musky cologne wafting past her nose. "Mr. Abbott has taken a special interest in Louisa since we arrived in London. You are fortunate not to be acquainted with him. He's as dull as pond water."

Matthew snorted, and she beamed at having elicited such a reaction. She returned her attention to Louisa as Mr. Abbott's squirrel-clawed hands grasped Louisa's gloves, no doubt scraping off the scales she'd so painstakingly painted onto the silk.

"I've been doing my best to keep them apart," Meg said. "You know as well as I how she cannot speak her mind when she is with people who make her uncomfortable. But the man is maddeningly persistent."

"Well he cannot be as persistent as you. No man could ever succeed against Meg Baker and her desires. That much I know."

Their eyes met. He was teasing her again, but his words brightened her hope. He was right. She had never been frightened to go after what she desired. Why should she be now? Of course, she did not know if Matthew had feelings for her beyond friendship, but it was time she discovered the truth.

She drew a deep breath. "Well, if that is true, then I think I shall leave you here to find a dance partner for myself."

He turned toward her. "You're really going to leave me here all alone?"

"What other choice have I, Matthew? I wish to dance."

She took a step away, but Matthew's words stopped her.

"Wait a moment. Suppose I make you a little wager?"

"You and your wagers," she said, feigning annoyance, though she was only amused.

Matthew had always loved making deals, ever since they were children. Their wagers ranged from Matthew reading Shakespeare with Meg if she stole pies for them to eat together, to seeing who could capture three hens before the other—the loser having to attempt to speak in French for the rest of the day. They were usually quite fair, though, and Matthew always saw to his end of a bargain, so she found herself not minding making deals with him.

"Very well, what do you have in mind?"

Clearly pleased with her willingness to play along, he replied. "I will dance with you again this evening if you remain in here until the next song begins."

Meg looked out at the dancers just beginning to form into sets. "They've not even started this dance though."

The mischief in his eyes grew.

"Oh, very well," she said. "We are in accordance then." She sighed, trying very hard to hide the fact that she'd received the better end of the bargain. "So, tell me. How was university? I've hardly—"

"There you are!"

Their eyes darted to the front hall where a tall, silhouetted woman stood before them. Her hands were on her hips, her back straight and head held high. "Matthew Charles Pratt. What do you think you are doing back here?"

"Good evening, Mother," Matthew said. He exchanged glances with Meg, his eyes shining, despite his mother's firm tone. They should've known Mrs. Pratt would find them.

Meg inadvertently took a step back. With how often she stayed at Hollridge House with Matthew and Louisa, Meg considered Mrs. Pratt a mother. The woman had always been kind to her, but Mrs. Pratt's sheer height—she was almost as tall as Matthew—made her a rather intimidating specimen. Nearly as intimidating as the fire in her eyes with which she now regarded her son.

"I ask you again," Mrs. Pratt said, "what are you doing back here?"

Matthew shrugged. "I thought it rather obvious. I'm merely enjoying Meg's company."

Meg pressed her lips together. Mrs. Pratt might be intimidating, but it was always humorous to watch Matthew talk his way out of his mother's many reproaches.

Mrs. Pratt huffed, leaning out of the corridor and motioning her hand in quick jerking movements to someone out of their sight.

Meg and Matthew exchanged glances, and Mr. Pratt soon appeared in the front hall behind his wife. As they moved forward, their faces finally became more visible.

Mrs. Pratt had lowered her disguise, her face every bit as red as the robin's mask attached to the stick in her hand. Mr. Pratt, dressed to match his wife, seemed more amused than anything.

"You see?" Mrs. Pratt said to her husband, tossing her head to Matthew. The soft brown feathers fluttered on the sleeves of her gown. "He is exactly where we thought he would be."

"Yes, I can see that," Mr. Pratt said.

Meg shifted her feet. This wasn't fair for her to remain in the background when she was the one to blame for their defection.

She took a step forward. "Forgive me, Mrs. Pratt, Mr. Pratt. I am also to blame for this. I wished to speak away from the crowds also, but I did not intend to…"

Mrs. Pratt shook her head. Her features softened as she turned to face Meg. "Oh, my dear. You mustn't think we are upset with you for a single moment. Matthew, however…" She glanced sidelong at her son.

Matthew held up his hands in defense. "Did you not hear Meg? She has all but admitted this *tête-à-tête* was both of our doing. I merely came along for—"

"Oh, do you ever stop your prattling?" Mrs. Pratt rested a hand over her closed eyes.

Matthew shot a devilish grin towards Meg, who shook her head in delight. He'd always received an inordinate amount of pleasure from teasing others.

"Now," Mrs. Pratt continued, "as you shall have plenty of time to visit with Meg over Christmastide, I do not think—"

"You will be spending it with us again?"

Matthew's eyes were on Meg. For a single moment, she wondered if he was unhappy with the fact that she would be with his family at Hollridge for the coming fortnight. But when his eyes brightened, her heart soared higher than the ballroom's lofty ceiling.

"Yes," she replied. "My parents are still visiting with the Malcolms in Scotland, so your mother has invited me to stay with you all."

"Excellent," he said.

Growing up, Meg had often stayed with the Pratts for the winter while her parents were with their friends, but last year, the Bakers had remained home for the holidays. Of course Meg loved her parents, but she far preferred a winter with the Pratts, and with Matthew.

She'd never seen him react so joyously to the news of her staying with them before. Did that mean she could hope that his time away at university had caused his feelings for her to blossom?

"Yes, yes," Mrs. Pratt said, interrupting Meg's thoughts, "we are all pleased she will be staying with us again. But do not think you can talk your way out of speaking with me, Matthew. You know I am displeased with your decision to hide away instead of performing your duty and dancing with the women in attendance." She turned to Meg, her brow smoothing. "And you ought to be dancing, as well, dear Meg. You worked too hard on that costume to waste it away in a dark corridor with my idle son."

She shot an accusatory look at Matthew, who responded with feigned offense. Meg fought off another laugh.

"Now go," Mrs. Pratt gently urged. "Find a partner worthy of your attention while I deal with this dilatory son of mine."

Meg hesitated. The last thing she wished to do was leave Matthew, but as Mrs. Pratt gave her one final, encouraging nod, she sighed. "Yes, ma'am."

She curtsied to the three of them then turned to depart. Mrs. Pratt did not wait to reprimand her son, her words reaching Meg's ears as Meg walked away.

"I am disappointed in you, Matthew," she said. "Tonight, your duty is to dance, not hide away. You may behave however you wish when you return to Oxford after Twelfth Night, but until then, you must do what…"

The words faded as Meg reached the dance floor. She wasn't sure if the brightness of the lights or Mrs. Pratt's words caused her head to ache the most.

Matthew was returning to Oxford. He would be leaving, again.

The hope she'd felt that night slunk back into the cage within her heart. Of course he would return to university. What reason had he to remain in Yorkshire?

Still, at the mere thought of him leaving again, panic clutched at her throat with iron fingers. How would she manage saying goodbye to him? How could she bear the coming months living with her feelings, all the while knowing nothing of his own?

She glanced over her shoulder, the white of Matthew's mask

glinting in the darkness as he listened—or rather, didn't listen—to his mother.

Two weeks was not long to ascertain his feelings, nor to fully understand her own. But Matthew himself said she was persistent. She could do this. She *would* do this. No matter how staggering the task, and no matter the outcome.

Matthew watched Meg disappear around the corner before he returned his attention to his mother.

"And then to keep poor Meg in here when she ought to be dancing? I thought I raised you better than that, son."

He blinked, trying to keep up with the conversation. A difficult task when his friend the doe looked so fetching that evening. In her defense, she always looked attractive.

Mother was right. He shouldn't have been keeping Meg with him when she really ought to be enjoying the masquerade. Yet, he couldn't chide his decision to take a moment alone with her. He'd missed her since saying goodbye October last, and he'd miss her again when the time came to return to university, but such was life.

"Are you listening to me?"

"Yes, Mother. I always listen to you."

She stared at him with jaded disbelief.

"I am," Matthew insisted, leaning against the side of the wall with his shoulder as he folded his arms.

He attempted nonchalance, though his chest tied in a knot at her look of disapproval. He didn't like to disappoint Mother, but honestly, she could do with a little lightening up, be a little more like himself and Father.

"What were you doing in here with Meg?" Mother asked.

"I already told you. I was merely speaking with her. Need I be hanged for conversing with an old friend?"

Mother did not send him another irritated look. Instead, she exchanged glances with Father. "So, you and Meg are…friends?"

"Of course she and I are friends."

He looked between his parents. Father eyes were averted, Mother's accusatory scowl missing.

"And there is nothing more between the two of you?"

He pulled in his chin. "More? Heavens, no." Where on earth was this coming from? He leaned forward. "Are you well, Mother?"

She pursed her lips, placing her hands on her hips once more. "Yes, I simply wanted to be sure. Does Meg see you as only a friend, as well?"

"Of course she...does..." His words lost steam before he could finish them.

He and Meg had always been close, even when he'd left for Oxford at eighteen, three years before. But nothing romantic had ever occurred between the two of them. He was sure she did not love him. But then, had she not asked him for another dance? Had her eyes not lingered on him a moment longer than they usually did?

No, the idea was preposterous. They were friends. They always had been, and they always would be. Mother was simply putting false notions into his head.

He ran his fingers through his hair. "No, you may rest assured. Meg and I feel nothing for each other beyond a dear friendship."

Mother stared at him, her expression unreadable until she nodded. "Very well. If that is true—"

"It is."

"—then I see no reason for you to be speaking with her in such seclusion, risking her reputation as well as yours."

He sniffed, brushing aside his mother's concern. "You worry far too much. I assure you, no one would think twice of childhood friends speaking together as we do."

"Prospective spouses might."

"Well, it is fortunate then that I do not intend to marry. At least, not right now."

He knew saying such words, though they were the truth, would upset his mother. She couldn't understand the fact that he'd not found a woman yet with whom he wished to spend the rest of his time on earth. That, and he was far too comfortable with his simple, carefree life right now to change it. He was happy with school as it allowed him respite from his mother's pestering. He was happy unmarried. He was happy without an estate to run. Mother would simply have to accept it.

Yet, she continued. "You do know your father and I will not be here forever, Matthew, do you not?"

Mr. Pratt chuckled. "Are you planning on either of us leaving this earth soon, my dear?"

"Of course not. I simply wish Matthew to take responsibility, to become the man he is supposed to be. To accept change when it comes. Even Louisa is doing her part, dancing with all the gentlemen this evening. She knows at twenty-one she ought to do her part to ensure she weds. Heavens, even Meg, three years younger, is doing better than Matthew." She shook her head in clear frustration. "I have failed as a mother. Our only son does not wish to marry. To produce an heir for Hollridge, carry on the family name, help you with the estate. What have I done to have earned such a burden?"

"Now, now, my dear," Father said with a warning glance to Matthew. "Matthew has said he does not intend to marry *right now*. We have every reason to have hope for the future. I'm certain as soon as he is finished with his education, he will also resume his place in helping me with the estate. As for now, you know I am more than capable and happy to continue on my own."

"Exactly," Matthew chirped in, which earned him another reprimanding glare from Mother. "I simply do not see the point in changing my way of life if I am happy with it. One day, I shall have all the responsibility you both have. Why not enjoy my freedom whilst I can?"

Mother brought her mask to her chin with the stick, rubbing the top of the disguise along her jawline as she stared at him.

An uneasiness skulked over him. His mother had never before held such a look of, well, plotting.

After another moment in silence, she finally spoke. "How about you and I make a little wager."

"A wager?" Matthew's brow lifted in surprise.

"I know how you enjoy them, a harmless bargain with very little risk."

With his interest piqued, Matthew glanced to Father, but he simply watched his wife with amusement.

Finally, Matthew agreed with a simple shrug. "Why ever not? What is it to be?"

"I promise to no longer pressure you to take a wife or to encourage you to help at Hollridge. In short, I will no longer interfere in your life."

"Indeed?" Matthew could certainly agree to that prize. "And what must I do to incur such a gift?"

Her lips curved. "All you must do is meet with nine women of my choosing from Christmas to Twelfth Night."

He narrowed his eyes. "And?"

"And, that is all. Apart from earnestly seeking to know each one of them as best you can."

Ah, of course. Now he understood. His mother's true plan was for him to fall in love with one of these women. Falling in love would force him to quit school, which in turn would bring him back to Hollridge where he would inevitably be drawn into taking over the estate.

Well, Mother would be disappointed. She may know him well enough to extend a challenge he could not refuse, but Mother, choose a wife for him? It was ludicrous.

Still, he would play her little game, if only for the fun of it. "Will not these nine women be upset if I show interest in one and then leave her for another the very next day?"

"No, I do not wish for you to hurt any of them, so you must seek to know them through *words* alone."

She gave him a pointed look, and Matthew nearly blushed. She was warning him not to kiss any of them. He ought to be offended. He'd kissed a few willing women in his life, but he was no philanderer.

"Of course," he said. "Through words alone."

"Very good. Now one last requirement. This wager will not be spoken of between anyone else but the three of us. Agreed?"

Matthew nodded. "I can manage that. Though, if I may ask, why nine? Why not make it a nice even number?"

She used her mask to flick back a curl. "I've never been fond of even numbers. Besides, my lucky number at hazard is nine."

Matthew pursed his lips then nodded. "Very well, Mother. I accept your wager."

Mother tapped her cheek. "Then you may seal our agreement now."

Matthew stepped forward and placed a kiss on her cheek.

"Now," she said with a raised chin, "I will leave to ensure Meg and Louisa are enjoying themselves with the men who *will* dance this evening."

With a curt nod, she turned, sharing a small smile with her husband before departing.

Matthew looked to his father, who remained behind. "You've been uncharacteristically quiet. Does that mean you disapprove of the wager?"

Father shrugged. "It wouldn't matter either way. Once your mother decides upon something, there is no use attempting to convince her to do otherwise."

Matthew blew out a breath. "She will be disappointed when I do not fall in love at the end of her little game. But I will be pleased to no longer have her pressuring me."

Father raised a brow. "So you do not think it likely that you will fall in love?"

"I know that I will not."

"So confident?" He clicked his tongue. "Your mother has always had the ability to read people well, son. And she has nine chances to find a woman who will be irresistible to you. I would be surprised if you don't fall in love before Twelfth Night."

Matthew barked out a laugh. "Ridiculous."

"Shall we make it a little more interesting then?" His eyes glinted brightly. "If you do not fall in love with one of the nine women before you return to Oxford, I'll fund your purchase of a new horse."

Matthew rubbed his chin with his thumb and forefinger. A

horse, now that was another prize worth fighting for. He grinned. "You have a deal, Father." He extended his hand, pausing. "You will not be requiring a kiss, will you?"

"A handshake will do, son."

They clasped hands, and Father stepped toward the ballroom. "Now, I must return to your mother's side before I receive a scolding worse than what you've just suffered." His chuckles filled the air as he disappeared around the corner.

Matthew adjusted his mask and moved closer to the ballroom, excitement simmering in his stomach.

What an excellent start to the holiday season this was turning out to be. He was away from the demands of university. He was reunited with his family, would be spending the holidays with Meg. And now, he would be winning his freedom from Mother, as well as a fine new horse from Father. Life just could not become any better.

With a deep, contented sigh, he absentmindedly watched the costumed dancers. His eyes found Meg in an instant as she danced with the squirrel, no doubt to save Louisa from the same fate twice.

His lips twitched at the sheer boredom on her face not even her mask could hide. He knew Meg enjoyed gentlemen who could keep up with her spry dancing, and the squirrel, frankly, could not. That was no doubt why she'd asked Matthew to dance again.

Well, he would sacrifice his dislike for the tedious pastime just this once, for the sake of his friend, and to make good on his deal.

After all, not even a lengthy reel could diminish his fine mood.

CHAPTER 2

Yorkshire

Y Meg stepped over the threshold of Hollridge House, striding out across the small landing. The brisk, morning air filled her lungs, nipping at her cheeks and fluttering the ringlets against her temples.

The musty scent of pine trees wafted toward her from the forest bordering the south side of the estate. She tried to draw in a deeper breath of the sharp aroma, but the thick air caught in her chest, the icy feeling spreading chills across her skin.

Her lips curled as she moved down the short steps of the house. This was what she'd been missing in London. The fresh air, void of smoke and soot. The silence of the countryside. The views of the green grass prohibited not by smog of factories and shops, but by the natural mist rising up over the hilltops.

More than anything, she'd longed for Hollridge House, a place far better than any exquisite townhome in London. She paused on the gravel drive, looking over her shoulder and sweeping her eyes across the home.

The blossom-red bricks stretched three stories tall with a brown roof and white columns at each corner. Ivy crawled along the left side of the house, and each window was bordered with ivory white frames. The house was not grand by any means, but the grounds were immaculately kept, the drapes were continuously parted, and the single front door to the house always appeared ready to open to friends and strangers alike.

How delighted Meg was to be back at the one place she truly considered home. Hollridge had always held far more of an appeal to her than her own house, Stoneworth Manor, with its gray edifice and narrow windows. The manor did not hold the same warmth and vivacity, no doubt due to its people.

Meg's brow pulled together, but she brushed aside the gloomy thought. Nothing would dim her mood this morning. It was Christmas Eve, and the festivities would shortly begin—just as soon as Louisa could pry herself out of bed and join Meg outside.

She looked toward the closed door. Where *was* Louisa? They were supposed to fetch the greenery for the house that morning. Though, knowing her friend, she would still be piling on her warm clothing. Louisa didn't find the cold as invigorating as Meg did.

An icy wind curved round the back of her neck, and she shivered, flipping the hood of her red cloak over her head. She peered up at the sky shrouded in thick, gray clouds. If they didn't begin soon, the rain would start. Being cold was refreshing. Being wet and cold was unbearable.

A click near the house drew her attention to the opening door, and Louisa finally appeared in the entrance.

"There you are," Meg greeted. "You have come not a moment too soon. We must hurry or the rain will set in, and…Why, whatever is the matter?"

Louisa moved across the landing, her lips drawn in a tight line. "*That* is what is the matter," she said, tossing her head backward.

Meg's eyes moved to the doorway as Matthew exited the house, securing the door behind him. Her heart fluttered. "Are you to join us this morning?"

Her voice sounded far too hopeful. She sent a quick glance to Louisa. Meg hadn't spoken to anyone about her growing feelings for Matthew just yet, and since she wasn't certain how Louisa would react to such news, Meg thought it better to keep the information to herself for now.

"Yes, my mother has insisted," Matthew responded. "She has decided to 'leave the traipsing around in the cold to the younger people this year.' Apparently, she still considers me a child while I am at home, so I must do her bidding."

Meg tried very hard to quell her delight. "Well, I'm pleased you'll be with us. We always do need another strong arm to help carry the baskets. Do we not, Louisa?"

Louisa folded her arms. "Yes, but must it be Matthew who helps us?"

Matthew sighed. "Oh, do calm down, Louisa. I was merely teasing you before."

Meg glanced between them. "Are you two quarrelling again?"

"Louisa has taken offense at a mere joke I have made."

Louisa moved to stand beside Meg, who watched the exchange with amusement. Usually, the twins were both jovial, especially during Christmastide, but four days confined in a carriage with a mercilessly teasing brother would set any sister on edge.

"Yes, a mere joke," Louisa retorted, her chin high. "But, like all of your joking, it was lacking in humor."

Matthew opened his mouth in mock horror. "I'll have you know I take great offense to that."

"Well, I meant it offensively."

Meg glanced to Matthew. "What have you said to her this time?"

"Nothing at all." His wink sent her insides fluttering each and every way, like a flurry of snowflakes in a soft wind.

"Do you truly think she will believe such a falsehood?" Louisa asked. "You cannot say a single word without teasing someone."

"Disagree," Matthew said, using, indeed, a single word to tease her.

She pointed her eyebrows at Meg. "You see?"

Meg held her muff closer to her mouth, attempting to hide her growing smile. As humorous as the scene was—and as much as it reminded her of their childhood—they couldn't waste any more time than they already had.

"Come now," she began, glancing between the both of them, "will you not set your quarrels aside so we may enjoy this morning together?"

Louisa closed her eyes and released a soft sigh. "You are right, dear Meg. It is good of you to remind us to forgive one another, as usual."

The girls looked expectantly at Matthew next. He raised both hands in a defensive pose. "I had no quarrel to begin with," he said. Then after a pointed look from them both, he dropped his hands. "Very well. I shall do my best to keep my comical comments to myself. For the morning, at least."

"Wonderful," Meg said, pleased at her ability to yet again smooth over one of the twins' disagreements.

Voices sounded nearby, and they turned to see a small group of servants—two housemaids and one footman—coming from around the house to join them. Their arms were filled with empty baskets and gardening shears. Together, their numbers were not spectacular, especially with Mr. and Mrs. Pratt not joining them this year, but there were enough of them to get the job done properly.

She rubbed her hands excitedly together inside her muff. This was one of her favorite traditions of the Pratts during the holidays. Her parents had always tasked the servants alone to gather the greenery and decorate Stoneworth, if they even chose to trim the house at all. Hollridge, however, was always filled to the brim with festive greenery and red berries.

"This should be everyone, Meg," Louisa said. Her voice was muffled as she raised her shoulders, her mouth disappearing behind her scarf. "Now do tell us where to go before I freeze to death in this awful cold."

Without Mr. and Mrs. Pratt there to take charge, Meg was the obvious choice, as Matthew did not typically join them for the activity and Louisa did not enjoy being assertive.

Meg, however, didn't mind. She stepped forward. "I think we ought to do the same as last year. Separate into a few groups to make the task swifter." The group collectively nodded. "Louisa, you and Harriet may gather the ivy and holly. Then you will be closer to the house for a quicker return."

A shiver wracked Louisa's body as she smiled at one of the housemaids.

Meg continued. "I'll take Grace and Colin with me to gather the hawthorn berries and evergreen branches. And Matthew," she turned toward him, forcing herself to focus on speaking rather than the soft dimples in his cheeks, "you go to the apple orchard and find what mistletoe you can growing on the trees. I spotted quite a large patch at the far east of the orchard, near the pear tree."

He lowered a single eyebrow. "You mean I must venture forth alone?"

Meg hesitated. She needed a man to carry the basket for her, as the pine branches would be exceptionally weighty, which was why she'd thought to bring along Colin. She would have suggested Matthew joining her instead of the housemaid and footman, but she didn't wish for Louisa to feel left out.

"Meg," Louisa said, as if reading her very thoughts, "I wonder if we should not leave him alone out there. What if he tries to eat one of the mistletoe berries? Then who would be here to tease us insufferably over the coming weeks?"

Matthew chuckled at her jibe. "Now who is teasing?"

"I have learned from the best." They shared a smile, evidence that all had been forgiven from before. "Truly, though, Meg. I think it would be best if you let Grace and Colin see to the mistletoe while Matthew helps you with the boughs. Knowing my brother, he is bound to do something wrong. You must keep him in check."

Meg laced her fingers together, suppressing the excitement bubbling within. This was all too easy. Louisa had practically dropped Matthew straight into Meg's lap.

Meg hadn't had much opportunity to speak with Matthew alone since the masquerade, but this would certainly resolve that issue. There was nothing untoward about the two of them going unaccompanied into the forest, either. They were dear friends, after all, and they had certainly been alone together before. Of course, she didn't have the feelings then that she now had for him, but no one needed to know such a thing.

"I suppose that will do," she said, slowing her words to avoid sounding too eager. "Will that suffice?"

Matthew's eyes shone. "I believe I can tolerate a few moments alone with you."

She looked away, fearing her fawning eyes might reveal too much of her feelings. "Shall we meet back in the drawing room when we have all finished?"

Louisa nodded, backing away with an impish grin. "I wish you luck with him, Meg. You most certainly will need it."

She spun on her heel before Matthew could respond. The housemaid Harriet scuttled along beside her as they made their way to the left side of the house.

Meg borrowed a pair of gardening shears and one of the baskets from the footman before she and Matthew headed south toward the woods.

"Isn't this lovely?" Meg asked as they walked across the grass beside each other.

Their breath floated around them in white puffs of air, their noses tinted red from the cold. The rain the night before had frozen to each blade of grass, covering them in frosted crystals. With each step, small pops echoed as the miniscule ice cracked beneath their boots.

"You are mad," Matthew said, holding their basket in front of him, the shears tucked safely inside. "No sane person could enjoy this cold."

She huffed. "You call *me* mad? What of your own sanity for teasing your sister?"

Matthew smiled, his lips taut from the cold. "I cannot help myself, you know this."

"Hmm. Will you now tell me what you said to her?"

"I was merely teasing her about Mr. Abbott. The squirrel."

Meg stopped. "Oh, Matthew, you shouldn't have. She's quite upset about the whole business. She'll hardly speak to me about him. He must have made her so uncomfortable the entire masquerade, following her around like a lovesick child." She shook her head. "Besides, you know she cannot bear your teasing. Quite like your mother."

"*Unlike* you," he returned.

She eyed him. Was he upset or pleased that she was not so easily frustrated with his teasing? Before she could decipher either, they reached the hawthorn trees standing at the edge of the woods.

The crimson red of the berries that pervaded every leafless branch contrasted radiantly against the dark green pines behind them. A gray robin with an orange breast stood perched on a low limb, its feathers puffing out to form a downy sphere around its body. As Meg and Matthew approached, the bird twittered out a trill whistle and took flight to a higher branch.

Meg paused beneath the first tree, looking up at the berries that dotted the clouded sky like red stars. "Would you mind cutting the branches higher up? They have more berries on them."

Matthew nodded and placed the basket on the ground. He reached up, using both hands to wield the shears. The snipping of branches and the pattering of Meg's boots as she collected the berries were the only sounds that broke through the silence.

After dropping her gathered handful into the basket, she straightened with her eyes on Matthew. He arched his head back, his thick scarf covering his neck, but she could just make out his angled jaw as he moved back and forth. Meg reached down and retrieved another branch, trailing her eyes across the contours of his chin.

"Is it to your liking?" he asked.

Yes, it certainly was to her liking.

"Meg?"

Matthew met her eyes. He raised his brow expectantly. "The branch," he said, motioning to her hand. "Is it filled with enough berries?"

Meg's eyes lowered to the bough of berries she waved toward her like a fan cooling down her face—an action she was entirely unaware of until that moment. Her cheeks stung, and this time, it was not from the cold.

"Oh, yes, thank you," she said in a rush, dropping the berries into the basket.

Matthew's eyes lingered on her for a moment before he resumed his cutting. He reached toward a higher branch, his voice strained as he stretched upward. "I take it you are happy to be returned to Yorkshire?"

"Yes, very much so."

"And you do not mind spending the winter away from Stoneworth this year?"

She regarded him inquisitively. "Have I ever minded such a thing?"

"Well," he paused, snipping off another branch, "I only wondered, what with your spending the holidays with your parents last year, if you wished to do the same again this year."

She sniffed. Since the Pratts had moved in, Meg had been dropped at their doorstep every winter so her parents could visit the Malcolms, childhood friends of Meg's father. The couple could not have children of their own, so Meg was never invited to join them. She was told she would be "too great a reminder for what the Malcolms could not have."

She had believed the excuse when she was younger, but now she knew better. Her parents simply did not want the responsibility of looking after a child, no matter the governess being tasked with most of the work when Meg was younger or how responsible a young woman Meg had grown to be.

Last year, however, the Malcolms had been ill, so Mother and Father had spent the winter with Meg. They hadn't bothered to decorate Stoneworth, nor did they attend any parties or gatherings, having Meg do the same. They'd merely remained indoors, feeling sorry for themselves for not being in Scotland. To have made matters even worse, Meg was only able to see the Pratts once or twice before Matthew returned to university for the term. It had been some of the worst weeks of her life.

She pushed aside the unpleasant memories, focusing instead on piling the berries into the basket. "If having my parents home during the holidays has taught me one thing, it is that I prefer them to be taken up with the Malcolms. They are far happier there, and I am far happier at Hollridge."

Matthew lowered the shears. "We are far happier with you here, as well."

She swallowed, their gazes catching. What was hidden deep within his hazel eyes? Love, friendship, or mere kindness?

"You know my parents have always considered you a daughter," he said, looking away to slice through another branch. "And Louisa and I have always thought of you as a sister."

A sister? So he saw her the same as he did Louisa. Of course, she should have known, but hearing the words aloud made her stomach twist and her hope to sink faster than the berries plummeting through the air, landing with a muted thud into the dirt below.

Matthew wanted to kick himself as he took in the sight of Meg's hollow eyes and turned-down lips. Why the devil had he brought her parents up? "I'm sorry, Meg," he murmured, picking up one of the branches he'd cut down.

She looked up at him. "For what?"

"For mentioning your parents."

Anger flamed within him, lapping at his throat. He couldn't understand the Bakers, their lack of responsibility, their lack of love for their only daughter. Of course, he was happy that Meg had spent so much time at Hollridge growing up. She was his dearest friend. But he couldn't bear the sadness her selfish parents evoked within her.

"I know how you dislike speaking of them," he said.

She ducked her head so her cloak's hood covered her face. "Things are better this year for both me and my parents."

He kept his eyes on her, the shears hovering below the branches. She was repressing her feelings again. Had her parents contacted her lately, said something to make her more upset than usual? Either way, he wouldn't press the issue any longer. He wouldn't have her become more upset.

"Have we enough berries, do you think?" he asked, motioning to the basket a third of the way full.

"Yes, this should do nicely." She looked beyond the hawthorn trees to the pines at the edge of the woods. "On to the evergreens then?"

He followed after her, noting her sunken shoulders and slower gait as her cloak rippled near her boots. He wanted his carefree friend back, the one who expressed her love for the cold, whose positive attitude always helped others to feel the same.

He reached her side, nudging her with his elbow. "Has the cold finally gotten to you?"

She gave him only a hint of a smile, the corner of her lips tucking in. "Perhaps."

The smell of the pines blanketed them as they reached the trees and weaved their way around the thick trunks and protruding roots. After deciding on a thick grove of low-hanging branches, Matthew followed Meg's directions as she pointed to which boughs to cut.

"I'm sorry your mother forced you out here in the cold," she said, setting the greenery in the basket atop the berries. "I'm sure this is not how you envisioned your time away from university."

"No," he said, "but I don't mind it. Especially the company."

There it was, the shining in her blue eyes, the soft curve of her lips.

He continued, his shoulders a little straighter, just like hers. "This is a welcome reprieve, though, I must admit. The classes were fairly easy this last term, but I suspect they will become more difficult."

"For how long do you aim to attend?"

"I haven't decided yet."

"Well, when you do finish, are you looking forward to helping your father with Hollridge and your tenants?"

He lowered the shears for a moment, returning the feeling to his arms. "I haven't really thought much about it. Besides, Father is doing well enough on his own. I would no doubt get in his way if I attempted to help him now."

"I don't believe that for a moment. You are very capable, Matthew." She didn't meet his eyes. "At any rate, I believe you are just delaying your duties. You never were one to have a thought or care for your future."

"That is true. I simply do not feel the need to plan ahead when my present is as perfect as I could ever wish it to be."

Meg gathered the pine boughs, laying them in her left arm as she watched him from the corner of her eye. "So you do not wish to change a single thing about your life?"

He stared inattentively at the pine needles strewn across the forest floor. Before moving to Hollridge House, his family had lived in a small home in Lincolnshire. When Father's distant cousin passed away with no heir, the Pratts sold their house, relocated their family, and moved to Yorkshire. Since then, Matthew had found it easier to live his life without plans or expectations than to have them disrupted.

Before university, he'd refused to decide between Eton or Harrow for college, so his parents—kindly not wishing to uproot his life again—had hired a private tutor instead. A few years later, Father had to choose Oxford for him, as Matthew did not wish to make plans to attend, on the likelihood that they might fall through.

Living such a way prevented heartache and disappointment and brought endless ease and comfort. How could he wish for anything more than that? Short of his mother ending her interference in his life, which he would finally have in a fortnight, his life was fairly perfect the way it was.

He shook his head. "No, I don't believe I'd change a single thing about my life and the way it is right now. I'm quite happy."

He expected her to congratulate him on his contentment, but she merely dropped the cuttings into the basket.

"That will be enough, I think," she said. "If we cut any more, you'll not be able to carry it back to the house."

He narrowed his eyes. "Are you questioning my strength after complimenting it earlier?"

"Perhaps."

"Very well." He extended the shears toward her, handles first. "If you will but hold these, I shall prove to you my strength."

She retrieved the shears, and he lifted the basket, letting out an exaggerated groan. "You see?" he grunted. "I am stronger than ten men combined."

A few branches slid off the top of the basket, and Meg bent down to retrieve them, keeping hold of them. "Yes, a veritable Hercules, you are." Her tone was still short, but her lips fought off a smile.

He took a few steps forward, hardly able to see over the mound in the basket. "If you will but direct my path so I will not plummet to the ground and wound my pride, I would forever be in your debt."

"Very well. Come along."

As they traversed slowly through the forest and over the grounds, Meg warned him when a root jutted forth, the grass dipped down, or another step was to be made, until they finally reached the warmth of Hollridge House.

He lowered the basket to the floor in the front hall as Meg closed the door behind them. He shrugged off his great coat and removed his gloves, handing them to a passing footman.

"There," he said to Meg, "you see how capable I am to have made it all that way without any…help?"

He looked back at her, her arms filled with more than a dozen large branches and the shears.

She raised her eyebrows. "You were saying?"

"Where in heaven's name did those come from?" he asked, posing his best innocent expression.

She shook her head, walking past him. "When you have recovered, bring those boughs to the drawing room, please. Louisa must have arrived already. She will have been waiting for ages, what with how long you took walking back with your little basket."

She disappeared down the side corridor without a glance back.

Matthew chuckled to himself. He'd always admired Meg's ability to brush off his jibes and deliver them right back. It was even more entertaining than Louisa and Mother's squirming.

"Matthew?"

He turned to his mother, who had seemingly appeared from his thoughts. She moved down the stairs at the right of the room.

"Good morning," Matthew greeted. "I trust you enjoyed the warmth of your bed whilst the rest of us suffered in the cold?"

"I did, thank you." She extended a folded piece of paper to him, lowering her voice. "Here, I believe you are in need of this. The nine."

His stomach twisted into knots, nine to be exact. Here was the list of women Matthew had agreed to come to know over the next couple of weeks. The nine women with whom he'd sworn not to fall in love.

A strange feeling washed over him. Whether it was regret for accepting the challenge in the first place or disappointment that it had already begun, he wasn't quite sure. Still, he accepted the note. "I must admit, I have been rather curious as to your choices."

She took a few steps away. "Now you remember, son. Not a word to anyone or the deal is forfeit."

He nodded. "Of course."

Without another word, she returned up the stairs, leaving Matthew alone in the front hall.

He brushed the note back and forth against his left palm, chewing the inside of his cheek. Was this truly how he wished to spend his Christmastide? To visit with women his mother wished for him to wed, rather than enjoying his brief time with his family and Meg, enjoying leisure activities, his time at home, eating what he wished, doing as he wished?

To win freedom from his mother and to win a horse from his father, yes, this was what he wished to do.

He swept his eyes about the room, ensuring he was alone before unfolding the note and eying his mother's tall, swooping script. The list was numbered one through nine. Matthew saw but one name, the first at the very top of the list.

He stiffened. "Meg?"

"Yes?"

His eyes flew up. Meg paused with one foot in the front hall, her cloak draped over her arm, her gloves halfway removed. His mind was a whirl. For the first time in his life, he hadn't a response. Her curious eyes flicked to the paper in his hands.

The paper. He needed to hide the paper. Swiftly, he folded it up and slipped it into his pocket.

"What was that?" she asked, motioning to where he'd hidden the note.

"Merely a list of tasks my mother wishes me to see to before I return to university."

He cringed. Tasks. What a word to use. What would these women think, knowing they were his *tasks*. What would Meg think?

Meg. Why on earth was she on that list? Did Mother wish Matthew to marry his friend, even after he'd denied any feelings for her? Or had Mother simply added the name to allow him an easy beginning to the job before him?

That must be it. That was the only logical explanation.

"Did you need something, Matthew?"

He looked up with a blank expression.

"You did say my name, did you not?"

"Oh, yes." He squeezed his eyes closed. "Yes, I was merely calling out for you as I forgot in which room we were meeting. I didn't wish to carry this basket any longer than necessary."

She didn't believe him. It was obvious by the pointed look in her eyes. Still, she responded. "In the drawing room. I was just returning my things to my room, and then we shall start on the kissing boughs."

"Right, yes," Matthew said, so distracted he hardly had time to notice her pink cheeks as she scurried past him.

He stared after her, rubbing at his temple. He wanted to pull out the note to read the other names, but he couldn't risk being caught again. He would simply have to wait until he dressed for dinner.

It was just as well. His thoughts were far too distracted with Meg being number one on his list.

Well, perhaps their time together gathering the greenery and creating kissing boughs would count toward Mother's bargain then? That was easy enough. And as he had not fallen in love with his friend—an absurd notion, really—his agreement with Father still stood strong.

He unwound his scarf from around his neck. This arrangement was turning out to be far easier than he'd expected. If the other women on the list were as easy as Meg had been, the next two weeks would fly faster than his new prized horse would.

He picked up the basket and headed to the drawing room, smiling as he imagined the horse races he would have against Meg in the summertime, as they did every year.

Perhaps planning for the future wasn't so very bad at all.

.

CHAPTER 3

*C*hristmas morning dawned early for those at Hollridge House. The bright sun cast its shining rays across the frozen landscape around them, causing the frost on the ground to shimmer and Meg's breath to glow as they loaded into the carriage for church that morning.

She glanced at Matthew, who sat across from her as they traveled toward Haxby. He stared out of the window. His hazel eyes glinted green in the sunshine before they focused on her.

He sent her a soft smile, a simple gesture, but Meg's heart thumped hard against her chest. She returned the motion and forced her eyes elsewhere. She couldn't spoil her plan now by becoming weak-kneed and glossy-eyed each time he looked at her. She was determined in her efforts this time.

The day before, as she and Louisa had hung up the kissing boughs, they'd giggled over whose affection they wished for that year. Meg had kept silent over whose lips she truly wanted to be on hers. She could never admit to those feelings aloud now, not when Matthew would kiss her the same as he did every year—on the cheek, just like he kissed his sister.

Sister. The word had all but flattened Meg's hope, like the

hawthorn berries she'd squished beneath her boots in the woods. After Matthew had spent all of Christmas Eve with her, however, decorating the house as they laughed and teased together, she knew she had some chance yet for his feelings to change.

After all, *hers* had. That knowledge, and the fact that Matthew clearly enjoyed his time with her, set her hope to blossom anew. She merely needed to show him how perfect they were for each other, then he would realize that he truly did love her. Or at least he would one day.

Perhaps she might then receive his affection under the kissing bough, affection that was not meant for a sister.

Soon, with Meg's cheeks rosy, they arrived at the church and huddled together in the box pew. Though she longed to be closer to Matthew, she was almost relieved to have Louisa seated between them. Otherwise she might not have been able to enjoy Mr. Kempthorne, the vicar, and his keen ability to share the first Christmas story without pomp and flare—but still without putting to sleep half the congregation.

When the service finished, the families filed out of the door, complimenting the gentleman on his words. Mr. Kempthorne stood tall with an endearing smile and kind eyes. Meg and Louisa had often spoken of how handsome the unmarried vicar was, but they'd always agreed that they enjoyed gossip and other worldly endeavors far too greatly to marry a man of God.

"Thank you for your sermon today, Mr. Kempthorne," Meg said with a curtsy as she followed the Pratts out of the church. "I always enjoy them."

The vicar bowed low in gratitude. She took a step away before his words stopped her. "I trust your parents are well, Miss Baker."

She glanced to the Pratts, who waited for her at the bottom of the stairs. "Yes, they are in Scotland again, as usual. I believe they are enjoying themselves."

She made to walk away again, but he continued. "I hope you are keeping warm in this cold weather."

Meg eyed him. Did he not realize the line of well-wishers behind her grew impatient with his extended conversation? "Yes, sir. The Pratts have been sure to keep me very comfortable, as always."

He opened his mouth again, but she curtsied. "Good day, sir," she said, then walked away before he could say another word.

A woman worthy of a vicar would never try to escape one. It was fortunate that she was in love with another man entirely.

She reached the Pratts below then looked from side to side. "Where has Matthew gone?" Meg asked, her brow puckered.

Louisa motioned behind her, and Meg followed her line of sight across the churchyard to where carriages lined the outside of the stone wall. Matthew stood near one of the carriages, speaking with the Paulsons, a family with a single daughter who'd just returned from boarding school in Hereford. Meg didn't know much about Miss Paulson, what with the woman living away from home for so long, but Meg did know that she was rather reserved.

"Why is he speaking with them?" Meg asked under her breath as she and Louisa followed Mr. and Mrs. Pratt toward their own carriage.

Louisa shrugged. "Wishing them the compliments of the season?"

Meg found that difficult to believe, especially by the look of pleasure on Miss Paulson's slender face, her cheeks glowing red. What had Matthew said to have instigated such a reaction? Or was it merely his dimpled smile causing her to blush?

"I did not know he was acquainted with Miss Paulson," Meg whispered.

"Nor I." Louisa's apathetic tone did nothing to settle the knot twisting Meg's stomach.

They entered the carriage and waited only a few moments before Matthew joined them. He settled down across from Meg, who tucked in her legs more securely.

"My apologies to have kept you all waiting," Matthew said as the horses jerked forward. "I hope no one objects to my inviting the Paulsons to dinner this evening."

Disappointment settled at the bottom of Meg's heart as cold as a block of ice. Every year for Christmas dinner, only the Pratts and

Meg had been present. Now, they would have to entertain another family with a single daughter who seemed rather taken with Matthew?

"I think it a fine idea," Mrs. Pratt said. "I understand the Paulsons have decided not to travel to family this year over the holidays. I'm sure they appreciate the invitation."

"Indeed," Mr. Pratt agreed. "A generous offer, son."

Meg looked away, holding her bottom lip between her teeth. She chided her uncharitable thoughts. The Pratts had always been a kind and welcoming family. They'd invited *her* into their home since the beginning. Of course, Matthew had never been one to extend his social sphere to many, but the spirit of the season must have prompted him to be more generous.

Meg ought to follow his example. "Yes, I'm sure we'll all enjoy their company," she forced out.

Louisa's eyes fixed on Meg, but Meg couldn't have her friend discovering her unhappiness with the Paulsons, particularly Miss Paulson, joining them. That would lead to questions she was not yet ready to answer. She simply shifted her lips upward and stared out of the window, forcing a pleasant demeanor, though her insides boiled with torment.

As the day progressed, she tried to focus on the holiday and the time she *did* have with the Pratts alone. The decorations around the house improved her mood, but only slightly.

Hollridge certainly was alive with the aromatic scents and festive sights of the season. Speckled with hawthorn berries, the evergreen branches were draped across the mantels of the fireplaces, hung over doorways, and propped atop window ledges. Ivy curved around every banister in the house, and multiple kissing boughs could be spotted in nearly every room that would be occupied in the coming weeks.

Despite the festivities, Meg's worries cultivated, her mind continually straying to Matthew's reasoning for inviting the Paulsons. Was he truly wishing to know Miss Paulson further? Or was he more interested in Mr. Paulson's talk of his horses? Either way, a single evening with the soft-spoken woman couldn't diminish the years of friendship that had flourished between Meg and Matthew.

At the thought, her hope renewed, and by the time Meg dressed for dinner, she was determined again to follow through with her plan. She would capture Matthew's attention that evening—and keep it away from Miss Paulson—if it was the last thing she did.

As such, Meg was eager to spend time with him alone before the other guests arrived, if only to solidify her place at the forefront of his mind. She rushed her lady's maid to tend to her hair as swiftly as possible, then dressed in her white gown with green sheer fabric lining the outside.

When the servant finally finished, Meg popped a peppermint drop in her mouth—the one sweet she couldn't abide living without during Christmastide—then bolted down the stairs and toward the drawing room, stopping momentarily to allow her breathing to level off before entering.

Matthew stood by the hearth alone, just as she'd suspected. He was always the first ready. He didn't like his valet to fuss over his hair or clothing as other men did, but he couldn't be more perfect to Meg if he dressed himself. He stood with his confident, yet casual stance, his face freshly shaved and cravat tied rather smartly beneath his chin. His red waistcoat finished off his striking appearance with a bright burst of color.

As she moved into the room, his eyes followed her. "I'm surprised to see you down here so swiftly."

She finished off the last of her peppermint drop. "What can you mean?"

"You and my sister are always the last to arrive. Constantly primping, you are."

She laced her gloved fingers together with a shrug, coming to stand before him. "Can you blame us for wishing to look our best?"

The right side of his lips lifted. "No, I don't suppose I can. You look lovely, at any rate, as always. And I see you have made good use of my clippings from yesterday." He motioned to her hair.

Meg raised a hand to softly press against the curls arranged in a pleasing manner at the crown of her head. Her lady's maid had dotted her blonde ringlets with the remaining dark red hawthorn berries.

"Do you like them? I didn't wish for any of the berries to go to waste, though I fear I resemble a tree."

He sniffed a laugh. "No, I believe you are safe in that regard." His eyes lingered on her for a moment before he looked toward the window.

Was he anticipating the arrival of their guests? Looking forward to it even? She tried to swallow, but her throat was dry, as if lined with the ash from the very fire they stood beside. "It was good of you to invite the Paulsons this evening."

He maintained his stare out the darkened window. "I'm glad you think so. I was worried you and Louisa would be upset with my inviting them. I know we three typically enjoy dining together with my parents alone on Christmas."

Meg couldn't pull back the question before it rolled off the tip of her tongue. "May I ask then, why *did* you invite them?"

He rubbed the back of his head. Why wouldn't he look at her? He was behaving as strangely as when she'd caught him with the note the day before in the front hall, the contents of which he'd been clearly lying about.

Before she could press him for an answer, Mr. and Mrs. Pratt joined them in the drawing room.

"Why, Meg, you're down here early," Mrs. Pratt said.

Matthew spoke from the side of his mouth. "You see? Even my parents know how long you take to make yourself presentable."

Meg brushed aside her musings, her mood lifting with Matthew's teasing.

Nearly a quarter of an hour later, Louisa made her appearance in the drawing room, followed soon by the Paulsons. Meg tried not to notice Miss Paulson's bright blue eyes lingering on Matthew, nor the way he strode directly toward her with a welcoming smile, bringing her at once to Louisa and Meg.

"I was just telling Miss Paulson how delighted we are to have her at Hollridge tonight," Matthew said, looking between his sister and Meg.

"Oh, yes. Indeed we are," Louisa responded with all the politeness Meg could not muster. "We do hope you enjoy yourself."

"Thank you," Miss Paulson said, her eyes flashing toward Matthew. "You are all too kind. Though, I do hope we are not intruding on your private party."

"Oh, not at all," Louisa responded. "We are so happy to have you here."

Meg wished very much to tell Louisa to speak for herself. Instead, she settled on something more appropriate. "You know as well as everyone in Haxby how kind the Pratts are, Miss Paulson. They are willing to share their home and kindness with anyone."

"Oh, yes, how very true that is," the woman agreed.

Meg stretched her lips into a sort of smile before she fell silent. She half-heartedly listened to the conversation until Mrs. Pratt announced that dinner was ready, and the small party filed into the dining room.

Any respite Meg had hoped to receive from her worrisome thoughts vanished as Matthew and Miss Paulson sat down across from her.

Suddenly, the brawn, Yorkshire puddings, roast goose, and six other dishes all placed on fine china and decorated with greenery appeared less appealing than a basket of poisonous mistletoe berries.

Still, she ate, if only to avoid drawing attention to her miserable state. From what Meg remembered, Miss Paulson had been a painfully quiet child. Being at school must have changed her, for she now proved to be quite the pleasant conversationalist. In fact, she was so agreeable, that Meg might have enjoyed her company, perhaps even counted her as a pleasant friend.

But the fact that Matthew spoke with Miss Paulson more than anyone else inevitably placed the woman at the top of Meg's "I would prefer to remain acquaintances" list—a list which, incidentally, she had created that very night.

As the meal progressed and the dessert course was finally served, Meg struggled to enjoy the layered trifle and apple dumplings she once so loved. Every look shared between Matthew and Miss Paulson, every smile he sent in the woman's direction, drove Meg closer and closer to madness. She listened in silence as the two spoke about their experience at their respective schools, and how difficult it was being away from home, until the women finally withdrew to the drawing room.

As Mrs. Pratt conversed with Miss Paulson and Mrs. Paulson about the upcoming Twelfth Night revels, Louisa's eyes constantly drifted toward Meg, but Meg hardly noticed. She was too busy concocting a number of excuses for Matthew's behavior, ranging from an instantaneous fever, to his simply playing the part of a good host, even to him being forced to speak with the woman.

But her musings were in vain. She knew the very reason he was speaking with Miss Paulson. It was the reason she feared most of all, a reason she refused to acknowledge until now. A reason that became more apparent when the gentlemen rejoined the ladies.

Matthew always came straight to Meg after port, but tonight, he headed in Miss Paulson's direction.

The action clicked something in Meg's mind, resounding within her like the snap of a broken twig in a silent forest. Her thoughts flew by in a whirl. She couldn't make sense of them, nor could she bear the sight of Matthew falling for another woman. What if this night was merely the beginning? What if Meg lost her friend forever? What if Matthew…married Miss Paulson?

Her panic shifted to indignation at the thought. Meg needed to do something before this nobody, this *Miss Paulson*, ruined her chances with Matthew and sabotaged her very happiness.

Without another thought, she jumped up from her seat and sailed toward Matthew, linking her arm with his and swiftly turning him away from the others.

"Why, Matthew, I'm so pleased to be reunited," she said, radiating sweetness.

He stared down at her in stunned silence. She felt as if two powers were struggling to gain control of her, one of sound sense, the other, nonsensical fear. Why was she speaking so loudly, and why was she holding onto his arm so tightly?

"Did you enjoy the port?" she asked.

"I always do," he said, still following her as she pulled him along.

She ignored his frown. "Oh, of course you do!" She belted out a laugh that would have sent her mother after her to chide her boisterous behavior.

Matthew halted their progression and stared down at her, speaking in a lowered voice. "Are you well?"

She patted his arm. "Why, of course I am, you silly. Why would I not be? It is Christmas Day, I am with my very dear friends, we have just had a marvelous meal, and I—"

"Why do you speak so loudly?" He glanced over his shoulder.

Meg froze. He was looking to Miss Paulson as if to see if the woman was watching Meg's actions. Was he embarrassed by her?

Finally—*finally*—her sense took over. In a single movement, she pulled her hand from Matthew's arm and took a step away. "Forgive me. I think I ought to sit down for a moment."

Her voice had returned to normal. She pressed a hand against her stomach, praying the food might remain within her.

"Are you certain?" he asked.

She merely nodded, turning her back on him and crossing the room in the direction of the window.

Being away from the blazing fire and the eyes of others, Meg breathed deeply for what felt like the first time that evening. She leaned toward the cold window, nothing visible but the frost framing the windowpanes.

She was a fool. An utter fool. How could she have allowed herself to act in such a way? Clearly her odd silence throughout dinner had been noticed—as evident by Louisa's earlier stares—for Meg was not typically silent during parties. And Matthew had certainly noticed her now, but for all the wrong reasons.

"Meg?"

She started, turning her head as Louisa approached.

"Are you well?"

Meg held the backs of her fingers to her cheek to quell her warmth further. "Yes, I am. I was feeling a little strange earlier. No doubt I ate too swiftly."

Louisa stopped in front of her, her voice soft as she spoke. "You and I both know that is not true."

"Whatever can you mean?" Her eyes involuntarily drifted toward Matthew. He sat next to Miss Paulson alone near the fire. Was Meg imagining it, or did they lean together in hushed conversation?

Louisa whispered, "I know my brother well, my dear friend. I like to think I know you well, too. Just as I know you aren't going to get his attention by behaving strangely."

Meg blanched, her stomach dropping to reside at the wooden floor beneath her slippers. Did Louisa know? Meg had tried to be careful in hiding her feelings. How could her friend have discovered her secret?

A warm expression enveloped Louisa's features. "I saw the change come over you the moment Matthew left again for Oxford. You blush when you speak of him and smile whenever his name is mentioned. You are in love with my brother."

Meg brought her hands to her lips. She'd tried so very hard to keep her feelings a secret, for her own sake, for Matthew's, and for Louisa's. She feared the truth might upset her friendship with both of them. But then, Louisa didn't appear upset.

She paused. "You are not unhappy?"

"Unhappy?" Louisa said in a louder voice. She glanced over her shoulder, continuing in a lower tone. "How could I be? My sweet, wonderful friend in love with my brother! We shall truly be sisters then."

Meg tried to keep her head afloat as hope and despair ran past her like the spring runoff in a raging river. "But he does not love me in return. He has said so himself when we were gathering the greenery on Christmas Eve. He thinks of me only as a sister."

"That is nonsense. We must simply help him to realize his true feelings for you."

"I have been trying but failing miserably at that task, I'm afraid."

Louisa flashed a smile. "That is because you have not enlisted the help of his sister."

"You will help me?"

"Of course I will."

The tension in Meg's neck slipped away. "I cannot express to you my gratitude, Louisa. I swear, I shall return the favor the moment you tell me that you love another."

Red swept across Louisa's face, but she shook her head. "Yes, well that will be a long time from now. Let us first focus on you. You must strive to behave like yourself, not this strange woman you've been, pulling him away from the others, being silent through dinner."

Meg nodded, her determination growing. "But Miss Paulson's reserved nature is proving to capture his attention. Perhaps I ought to behave the same."

"Heavens, no!" Louisa whispered with an exasperated sigh. "She is a terrible bore. If I have her for a sister-in-law, I shall fall asleep each time she tries to speak with me."

They shared a stifled laugh. "It is fortunate Mr. Kempthorne is not with us to hear you speak such uncharitable words," Meg said, referring to the vicar.

"Indeed," Louisa agreed. "But you know Miss Paulson would never do for my brother. *You* most certainly will. Be yourself, Meg, the woman Matthew already adores. Then we shall work together to make that adoration turn to love."

Meg could hardly contain her joy. She wrapped her arms around her friend. "Oh, Louisa, what would I ever do without you?"

Louisa returned her embrace. "As evident by tonight, you would clearly behave like a mad woman."

They burst into another fit of giggles, not caring that they drew every eye in the room.

CHAPTER 4

*T*he next morning, Matthew rubbed the sleep from his eyes with his palms as he lumbered down the corridor from his room. He'd barely managed to roll himself out of bed that morning. Making an honest effort to better know Miss Paulson had made for a weary Christmas, indeed.

The woman was kind, well-mannered, and quite regal. But his witty comments had failed to produce a single laugh from her all evening. He would have far preferred spending Christmas with his family and Meg. At least *they* appreciated his humor. Occasionally. Meg more often than any of them.

He reached the top of the stairs and pressed a fisted hand to his mouth as he yawned. Perhaps he ought to admit defeat already and simply accept Mother's interfering in his life for a few years longer? Or perhaps he ought to fix her unhappiness by no longer hiding from her at school, by coming home and accepting the daunting responsibility of changing his life, running an estate, and marrying?

He scoffed under his breath. No, he wasn't ready for that. Besides, he couldn't give up after only one evening. Though, he had no idea how he was going to carry on in such a way with seven more women.

Laughter drifted toward him as he descended the steps—Meg's laughter. His lips raised. If the remaining seven women were as enjoyable as Meg to be around, he'd have nothing to worry about, but something within told him that he had the hardest work still ahead.

He neared the landing of the staircase, finding her buttoning her pelisse next to Louisa in the front hall. Skates rested at their feet, and they leaned close to each other, speaking in hushed tones like the night before in the drawing room.

Matthew still couldn't make sense of Meg's silence throughout the evening, then her uncharacteristic outburst as she pulled him away from the others. He figured she was unhappy with the Paulsons joining them, though she'd always enjoyed larger parties, unlike himself. Fortunately, after the moments she'd spent with Louisa, whispering in the corner of the room, Meg had returned to her usual, cheerful self. Though, he still wondered what Louisa had said to make Meg happy once again.

"Good morning, ladies," he greeted as he approached.

They turned in unison toward him. "Ah, you have finally risen, I see," Louisa said. "We've been awake for ages, you know."

"You can't expect me to remain this dashing without a few added hours of sleep," he said, running a hand down his waistcoat.

Louisa and Meg exchanged amused glances. "I suppose we shouldn't be too surprised with your idleness," his sister continued. "You must have been exhausted after your efforts last night."

"Efforts?"

"With Miss Paulson."

Both she and Meg looked away. Were they upset that he'd abandoned them last night for Miss Paulson? He would not wish them to be offended, but he couldn't forfeit his agreement with Mother by telling them why he'd truly focused on her.

"I paid no special effort to her," he lied. "I was merely being a gentleman."

The girls shared another glance. He narrowed his eyes. What were they scheming? And why was Meg not speaking again?

"Will you be seeing Miss Paulson today?" Louisa asked.

Finally, understanding dawned. Of course. They'd imagined an attraction between him and Miss Paulson. He opened his mouth, ready to feign falling in love with the even-tempered woman to tease his friend and sister, but his conscience prevented him. The rumors Louisa was sure to start could hurt Miss Paulson. Though he'd set about refusing to fall in love with any of the nine women, he'd also determined not to harm them.

Truth would be his best route. "No, I will not be seeing Miss Paulson today, nor do I have any plans in the future to do so."

Louisa blinked, Meg's eyes swung up.

"Is that true?" asked his sister.

"Yes, it is."

Matthew was fairly certain he wasn't supposed to see the subtle nudge Louisa then gave Meg, who cleared her throat and spoke for the first time that morning.

"In that case, perhaps you'd like to join us skating," she offered. "Since the help are off due to St. Stephen's day, we thought it would be a fine way to pass the time."

Matthew rubbed his chin. He needed to see to number three on his list—Miss Michaels, he believed it was—but certainly after last night he deserved a bit of enjoyment.

"Yes, I will join you. Just one moment while I fetch my coat."

"You'd best hurry," Louisa said as he walked away. "We'll not wait for long."

He looked over his shoulder. "I know Meg would never be so unkind as to leave without me."

He caught sight of Meg's smiling eyes before he rushed back up the stairs.

Shortly, with their gloves, scarves, and hats donned, the three of them made their way to the pond, only a short distance past the woods near Hollridge. The small body of water was surrounded mostly by frozen grass, though thickets of trees edged a few stretches of the bank.

The pond had always been an attraction to many during the winter months, so the Pratts had opened their land to any who wished to skate. Already, a few couples slid across the ice together, and a small group of children huddled near each other at the far edge.

Matthew sat down beside Louisa and Meg on a thick log. They strapped their skates to their boots securely then ventured forth across the ice.

After a few laps around the pond, Matthew's legs grew used to the slippery feel of the ice beneath his feet, and the three of them were soon sailing smoothly alongside each other. Well, he and Louisa were. Meg still wobbled back and forth. She'd always been more unstable on the ice than he and Louisa.

"Isn't it lovely to skate again?" Louisa said. "Such an activity makes this cold nearly tolerable." She appeared to be in her own world as she skated away with a bright smile on her face.

Matthew glanced down at Meg, her arms held slightly out to the sides, a look of concentration on her brow.

He grinned, slowing his pace to remain at her side.

"If you wish to skate ahead, you may," she said.

"And leave you after you waited for me? I think not. Besides, someone ought to remain here by your side so you don't fall."

She pressed her lips together, clearly trying to hold in her smile. "I am perfectly capable of remaining upright."

"Of course you are." Her eyes were trained on the ice beneath them. He reached out, raising her chin. "If you look up, you may have better balance."

She looked toward him, then hurriedly pulled her attention forward. "But what if I trip on an unsuspecting branch?"

"You can't. The pond is clear of all debris."

They skated a few more strides, and Meg's posture straightened, her chin level with the ice.

"There, that's better, isn't it?" he asked.

They moved alongside each other in silence. Louisa was halfway across the pond, greeting a couple who moved slowly with their hands intertwined.

"Wouldn't it be lovely to be a bird?"

Matthew looked back at Meg, releasing a surprised chuckle. "What?"

"A bird." She motioned to the four birds calling and swooping overhead. "It would be rather freeing to soar through the air like that."

He'd always loved Meg's free spirit. If only he could make her wish come true. At his next thought, he stopped skating and reached his right hand toward her. "Here."

She stopped beside him, her body tipping to one side before she settled herself. "What?"

"You said you wished to fly."

"Yes, but that does not explain why holding your hand will allow me to do so."

He wiggled his fingers toward her. "Trust me."

She bit her bottom lip, hesitating a moment longer before she placed her hand in his. "Very well, but if you sprout wings and lift me toward the sky, I must warn you, I shall die of shock."

"As would I. But not to worry. We'll stay grounded."

He spun about in the same spot slowly, holding his arm outstretched as he spun her in wider circles around him, his body as the axis, her skates pointed forward. Gradually, he picked up his speed.

"I don't feel like I'm flying, but I do feel nauseated," she said, holding out her opposite hand to keep her steady.

He grinned, holding fast to her glove. Meg began to laugh, and he joined in as they continued in steady circles, their speed slightly increasing.

"I'm going to fall over!" she said with glee.

"Then we must act quickly. I will count to three, and then you shall fly."

Fear flashed in her eyes. "No, don't let go! I'm too afraid!"

"Letting go is the only way to fly. And you, Meg, are not frightened of anything."

Slowly, determination replaced the hesitance in her eyes, and she nodded firmly.

His heart warmed at her trust, as if a scarf had been wrapped around his chest. "One."

Her smile grew.

"Two."

She squealed, her teeth clenched together, and he laughed before finishing his countdown.

"Three!"

They released hold of each other's hands. Matthew instantly leaned forward to maintain his balance, taking a moment to stop his eyes from spinning before focusing on Meg. Her laughter sailed out as she flew across the ice away from him—until she teetered on her skates. He envisioned her fall before it could occur, and he sailed toward her. "Meg!"

Her arms flapped up and down to catch herself, like a small bird attempting its first flight. She yelped, then fell flat on her backside, sliding in a half circle until she came to a stop in the thick mud at the edge of the pond.

Her laughter sounded above the scratching of his skates against the ice. Thank goodness. She was well.

"Meg, forgive me," he cried out, reaching her side and moving at once to his hands and knees. "I thought you were balanced enough. I should've been more careful."

She waved a hand in the air, still laughing.

He struggled not to join in. "You are not hurt?"

"Only my dignity," she finally breathed out.

He stood, sighing with relief as he reached his hand toward her. "Allow me to help you up."

She accepted his offer, and he pulled her swiftly upward, holding her arms until she was firmly settled on the ice.

"You know, with all your flapping, I was fairly convinced you were to take flight after all."

Laughter burst out from her lips, though she tried to scowl. She reached out, making to swat his arm, but he raised it in a defensive position. She gasped, missing his arm entirely and falling forward.

He caught her against his chest, laughing. "You really are a nonsensical creature."

The smell of peppermint drifted toward him as she scrambled away. She wiped the tendrils of hair from her cheeks, her face red from the cold. They were too comfortable with each other for Meg to blush around him.

As she brushed at another strand of hair, mud streaked across her brow. With amusement, he reached forward to help dispel the mess, but she pulled back with a jerk.

He hesitated. Why had she reacted in such away? "I was merely wiping the mud away from your face."

"Oh," she said, doing so herself with her glove. "I no doubt have it covering my pelisse, as well."

He suspected for a moment that she would wish to return inside, either because she was sore from her fall or upset that mud had ruined her clothing. Instead, she turned toward him with bright expression.

"So, would you care to help me fly again?"

He shook his head with delight. "You are simply begging for punishment, my friend. But I promise to not spin you so greatly this time."

They skated toward the center of the pond, but before they could circle once, Matthew heard Louisa calling his name from behind.

He turned to see her pointing toward the bank opposite them, and Matthew followed the direction before his eyes settled on Mother standing at the edge of the ice with Mrs. Michaels and Miss Michaels at her side.

His neck tightened, as if the comfortable scarf was now stuffed down his throat.

"Is that Mrs. Michaels and her daughter?" Meg asked.

"Yes. It most certainly is."

Why was Mother bringing number three on his list to the pond, encroaching on his time of comfort? Did she not know how exhausted he was from the night before? Was it not up to him when he would see each woman?

He couldn't wait for his list to be completed. He would finish off one final term at school, then return to Hollridge to live out his days comfortably with his family and friend—and without Mother's constant meddling.

"I wonder what they can want," Meg said.

"I haven't a clue," he lied, then he skated forward, knowing full well what his mother wanted of him—and what he truly did not wish to do.

Meg stared after Matthew as he skated skillfully across the ice. She wondered why his mother's presence had induced such a reaction from him, his shoulders falling forward, the smile fading from his lips. Unless, of course, it wasn't Mrs. Pratt who had elicited such a reaction, but Mrs. Michaels and her daughter, instead.

She puckered her brow. The timing of their arrival was certainly not ideal. Things had been going so well between her and Matthew, despite her falling on the ice.

"Are you hurt very much, Meg?" Louisa asked as she skated toward her, glancing at her departing brother. "I saw you'd fallen but thought Matthew could take care of you far better than I could."

The twinkling in her eyes bore an uncanny resemblance to Matthew's. "He was rather attentive," Meg said with an airy sigh. "Though I can feel a bruise forming already where I fell."

"Surely the wound was worth it?"

"Of course it was."

They shared a knowing smile before they both turned to watch Matthew reach the bank. Meg and Louisa had hatched a plan the night before to go ice skating this morning, as Matthew had never been able to say no to the activity. But it was Louisa alone who had decided to ask after Miss Paulson. His denial of seeing the woman again had given Meg the hope she'd needed to invite him along with them. Though, she still wondered why he'd paid such close attention to Miss Paulson in the first place.

"What is *she* doing?"

Meg drew her mind back to the present, following Louisa's line of sight to Matthew, who was skating toward them, Miss Michaels at his side.

Miss Michaels and her family had just moved to Haxby last spring to open an apothecary shop. Meg didn't know much about her, only that Miss Michaels was rumored to have a large dowry funded by a doting grandmother—and that the young woman could often be seen pressuring customers to purchase more than they needed. Those customers were seen more often than not bending to her ever-convincing will.

"This is my mother's doing, I'm sure of it," Louisa said quickly under her breath.

Meg's concern grew. She knew all too well of Mrs. Pratt's desire for Matthew to settle well and to take his place beside his father at Hollridge. Meg also knew how resistant Matthew was to her pressuring. So why was he accepting her coercion now?

Before Meg could think further on the matter, Matthew and Miss Michaels were upon them.

"Good morning, Miss Baker, Miss Pratt," Miss Michaels said, skating toward them.

After half-curtsies were given—Meg wasn't stable enough to give a correct one—Matthew spoke up.

"Miss Michaels and her mother were calling at Hollridge. Mother told them we were here, and she—"

"Oh, yes!" Miss Michaels interrupted.

Meg jumped, starting at the loud voice that exuded from her small frame. The woman's head barely stood taller than Meg's shoulders, yet her voice croaked louder than the toad Matthew had brought into church as a child during a silent service.

Miss Michaels continued. "When I heard you were out here ice skating, I simply begged Mrs. Pratt to allow me to join you. I love ice skating! I was not even aware such a pond existed. Mind you, I shall be out here every winter now."

"Wonderful," Louisa muttered with a strained smile.

"She let me borrow an extra pair of skates, too," Miss Michaels continued, pointing at the skates strapped to her boots. "I do love the sport. Oh! Mr. Pratt, I saw you just earlier spinning Miss Baker round and round. I think I should like to give that a try, as well."

Annoyance poked at Meg. She glanced to Louisa, whose half-hooded eyes revealed how unimpressed she was with the woman. Meg wondered what had come over her friend. Perhaps all of her politeness had been used up with Miss Paulson the night before.

"Oh," Matthew replied with a glance at Meg, "I fear I'm a touch too dizzy from the last turn. Perhaps later?"

Miss Michaels folded her arms and looked away.

Meg tried not to feel too pleased with Matthew's decline. She fancied he did so because he didn't wish to fly with anyone other than Meg, though it was rather more likely that he *was* too dizzy.

Miss Michaels's pouting did not last for long as she turned toward them with a brightened smile. "Oh, I know! Let us have a race then!"

Without awaiting a response, she cupped her hands over her mouth and shouted toward the group of children. "You, there! Can one of you count for us?"

Meg jumped again at her brash tone, grasping onto Louisa's arm to steady herself on the ice.

The tallest boy skated toward them. "I'm happy to count for you, miss."

"Excellent, my good sir. On three, we shall go. Well, come on then, let us not wait for the ice to thin."

Meg exchanged looks between Louisa and Matthew before they hesitantly lined up beside her.

Miss Michaels pointed to a cluster of pines. "The finish line will be just beyond that tree there. Begin counting, young master."

She hunkered low, one arm in front, the other in back. Meg would've been entertained with her enthusiastic behavior, had not it interrupted the pleasant moment she'd been having with Matthew.

The tall boy raised his hand overhead. "One, two—"

Before he finished, Miss Michaels shot away from the others with a cackle. "Come along then! You must move faster if you wish to beat me!"

"I didn't say three yet," the young boy said with a perplexed brow.

Matthew shrugged, thanking the boy anyway, then sailed toward Miss Michaels with his long stride.

"Cheater," Louisa muttered. "We should've known. Aggressive, little…"

Meg held her own complaints, Louisa doing enough for the both of them as they moved slowly forward. There was no reason to increase their speed, what with no chance at winning.

"How could mother even think this woman was right for Matthew?" Louisa asked, shaking her head before they reached the others.

Meg's good mood sunk further. Indeed, how could Mrs. Pratt believe such a thing? More importantly, did she not think Meg was good enough to marry her son?

Miss Michaels reached the trees, turning around at once with her hands in the air. "I am victorious! Not even the great Mr. Pratt could defeat me!"

Matthew skated up beside her. "Well done, Miss Michaels," he said as Meg and Louisa reached the both of them.

"Yes, well done," Louisa mumbled. "If that were a fair race, of course."

Meg's eyes rounded. Louisa was never one to confront another on a delicate matter. She was far more comfortable speaking courageously in a whisper, with no possible chance of being overheard. What was she doing now, calling the woman out on her misguided actions?

Miss Michaels set her hands on her hips. "That *was* a fair race."

"Was it? Because I was certain—"

"Louisa," Matthew interrupted. "Perhaps you and Meg ought to skate together for a moment."

Meg froze. She and Louisa stood by in stunned silence.

Matthew's signature smile was gone. His tone was short, and his eyes held a subtle warning to them. His gaze flitted to Meg for a single moment before he held out his arm toward Miss Michaels. "Shall we?"

Miss Michaels looped her hand through his, and together, they skated away from Meg and Louisa.

What had come over him to behave in such a way, and to choose

Miss Michaels's side over his own sister's? She glanced to Louisa, noting the tears in her green eyes.

"Perhaps you are better off without my brother for a husband, Meg. Especially if he chooses that woman over either of us."

A cold draft seeped through Meg's pelisse and bonnet. Was he truly choosing Miss Michaels, or was Mrs. Pratt choosing for him?

Meg folded her arms. "I'm certain he's merely tired. That is why he is behaving so strangely."

Her words were hollow, even to her own ears. She looked over her shoulder to see Mrs. Pratt still standing at the edge of the pond, Mrs. Michaels at her side.

Mrs. Pratt waved toward them with a smile, and Meg weakly returned the gesture before Mrs. Pratt returned her attention to Matthew and Miss Michaels on the other side of the pond, the smile on her face telling Meg everything she needed to know.

Mrs. Pratt wished for her son to marry.

But she didn't wish for Meg to be his wife.

CHAPTER 5

*M*atthew had never been more relieved to see Hollridge House, even when he and Meg were children, being chased to the door by two crazed hounds. That experience, at least, had been exciting, once they were safely indoors. What he'd just gone through with Miss Russell had been mind-numbingly dull.

Miss Russell, number four on his list, was similar to all the women Mother had chosen for him—pretty, kind, and inherently good. But just like with Miss Paulson and Miss Michaels, Matthew had nothing in common with Miss Russell.

He was only supposed to have called that morning for a half hour, yet somehow, Miss Russell had convinced him to tour around the old churchyard in Haxby, close to the Russells' small cottage near the edge of town. Matthew had spent over an hour in the bitter cold and the freshly fallen snow, listening to the woman blather on about her relatives buried in the churchyard, quoting scripture after scripture about life and death.

Matthew didn't recognize half of what she recited, though that may have been more a testament to his own lack of knowledge of the Bible rather than the woman creating her own verses. What he'd really wanted to do in those moments was call for Mr. Kempthorne to join them. Most women seemed to think the vicar was attractive, and he would certainly have appreciated Miss Russell's knowledge of the scriptures far more than Matthew had.

He tightened his scarf around his neck to keep the wind from chilling him further, passing by a milkmaid bundled from head to toe in a ratted cloak and warn boots. She smiled as she walked on, humming a tune despite the cold weather.

Matthew could never understand how people—Meg included—could enjoy themselves in such bitter cold. Even as much as he enjoyed riding, he couldn't wait to be indoors, to sit before a blazing fire with a cup of piping tea, and to finally receive a break from crossing the women off his list.

After having a much-needed word with Mother about her ambushing him on the pond with Miss Michaels, Mother had agreed to take a step back, so long as she could simply suggest the activities and when to do them. Matthew had accepted, heeding her recommendation to call on Miss Russell that morning. To combat his fatigue over socializing, however, he'd decided to give himself time away from the bargain until New Year's Eve. That gave him three days of blissful peace and freedom to do whatever he wished and be with whomever he wished.

At the thought of his newfound liberty, though temporary as it was, his shoulders straightened, and the saddle he sat upon didn't feel as cold as before, nor did the wind biting his cheeks.

In fact, the snow looked rather pretty falling down around him, especially up against the backdrop of Hollridge's red bricks. The tops of the ivy leaves on the house were iced with flakes, as well as the bushes near the landing.

He should really find Meg and bring her outside. She always enjoyed the beauty of falling snow. In truth, he was surprised she was not out there already with her—

The front door opened, and a smile pulled across his lips. There she was.

Meg slipped out of the house, moving across the landing with her eyes cast toward the clouds so Matthew remained unnoticed.

When he'd spoken with his mother the day before, he'd asked what had possessed her to place Meg on her list.

"I simply needed an extra young lady, and Meg was the first to come to my mind," she had said. "Better her than your sister."

She'd laughed at her own teasing, though Matthew couldn't help but wonder if Mother still suspected him of having feelings for his friend. What gave her such an idea was beyond him. He and Meg had both remained unchanged over all these years, as had their friendship.

Even now, Meg looked and behaved just as she had when she was a child. She wore no covering other than her long-sleeved dress, evidence that her impulsivity from childhood had not yet faded away. The snowflakes floated around her, her hand stretched toward the sky before a smile graced her lips. She still had that ability to enjoy simple matters, to find beauty in everyday moments—an ability that brought joy to those around her. Matthew was sure he'd even enjoy the graveyard if Meg joined him there.

His horse snorted beneath him, jingling his reins, and Meg looked toward him in surprise. "Good morning, Matthew. I didn't see you there."

"Apparently." He pulled his horse to a stop and motioned to her shoulders. "Where is your cloak?"

She looked down at her dress, as if only aware in that moment that she wore nothing else. "Oh, I didn't have a moment to spare to retrieve it. I wished to see the snow falling before it stops again."

Just as Matthew had suspected.

A groom approached, and Matthew dismounted, handing the reins over with a nod of thanks before removing his hat and walking toward Meg. "Aren't you cold?"

"Not yet."

His eyes wandered toward the door. The blazing fire that was sure to be burning in the drawing room hearth was calling for him, but he was fairly certain if he left Meg alone, she'd remain out of doors until she caught a cold.

He removed his coat and ignored the chill instantly enveloping him as he wrapped the cover around Meg's shoulders.

"Thank you," she said softly, her fingers curling around the lapels as she pulled the coat tightly around her. "Won't you be chilled though?"

"I assure you, I could not be any colder than I already am. I may as well give you my jacket, gloves, and scarf."

"Well, what did you expect, riding in such weather? To return home stifling hot, breaking a sweat? Gaining a freckle or two?"

"I'll have you know, I had planned to be in the warmth of the Russells' home, but for some forsaken reason, Miss Russell preferred spending an eternity in the churchyard with the headstones."

Meg dropped her eyes to her boot as she pressed it in front of her, creating a small indent in the snow. "You called on Miss Russell?"

"On her family, yes," he corrected. The last thing he wished for was for Meg to think he was interested in Miss Russell. She would undoubtedly tell Louisa, and he couldn't have the two of them scheming together about him with yet another woman. "My mother was not feeling up to calling in this weather, so I offered to go in her stead."

There, that wasn't entirely a lie.

"Does your mother like Miss Russell?"

"I would think as much as any young woman."

"What of Miss Michaels? And Miss Paulson? Does she like them?"

"I suppose." He lowered his brow. Meg couldn't know about their agreement, could she? "Why do you ask?"

She shrugged, holding out her hand as the snowflakes speckled her palm. "Merely curious."

She seemed innocent enough, but perhaps that was due to the cold preventing his mind from working properly. He rubbed his hands together. Perhaps he'd be better off deducing the answer in front of the fire. "Are you ready to return indoors now?"

She tilted her head back, squinting as the snowflakes fluttered around her face. "No, I think I'll enjoy myself out here for a moment longer. If you wish to return indoors, though, do not let me stop you."

"Can I not even tempt you with cakes and tea?"

"Mmm. Indeed you can. But in a moment."

He folded his arms, his fingers beginning to ache from the cold, despite his gloves. Perhaps they could both last outside longer if she had her cloak, then he could ask for his coat back.

"I'll be back in just a moment."

He turned on his heel, making for the door, but before he could even reach the landing, something hard crunched against the back of his jacket.

He whirled around as Meg shook her hands free of the excess snow she'd used to create her snowball.

"What did you do that for?" he asked, peering over his shoulder at his back sprinkled with icy snow.

Meg shrugged, his coat sleeves flapping back and forth at her sides. "To repay you for leaving Louisa and I alone at the pond yesterday."

Matthew scoffed. Along with his mother the day before, he'd also spoken with Meg and Louisa, apologizing for dismissing them as he'd done on the ice. How he wished he could share with them the bargains he'd made, how pressured he'd felt with Mother's eyes on him from the banks, how he wished to remain with his sister and friend.

Instead, he'd blamed his shortness on a lack of sleep. Louisa had taken a bit of convincing, but Meg had forgiven him instantly. So how did she now think she could get away with throwing a snowball at him?

"I already apologized for that," he said, moving back down the landing.

"I know. It was also for this morning. How could you forget our plans?"

He stopped, guilt pinching his chest. He'd agreed to go to the bakery in Haxby with Meg and Louisa that morning. How *could* he have forgotten? Blast this bargain.

He placed a hand to his temple. "My apologies, Meg. I don't know how I managed to forget. We can go this very moment if you wish to."

"And risk having to hear you lament about the cold for longer? I think not."

Her lips twitched. Was she fighting off a smile?

He took another step toward her. "I will make it up to you both. Why do we not walk there tomorrow? And for the next three days, I'll do whatever Louisa and you wish to do."

He'd have to say farewell to his freedom if she agreed, but the prospect wasn't all bad. At least whatever Meg decided for them to do was sure to be more fun than speaking of deceased ancestors in a frozen graveyard.

Meg nodded her head in an instant. "Very well, you have yourself a deal, Matthew."

He ran his fingers through his hair. He'd never made so many deals in his life than he'd had that Christmastide. Fortunately, he knew this one he could accomplish with as much ease as he was accomplishing Father's.

Besides, hadn't Mother's bargain said to spend time with those on the list between Christmas and Twelfth night? He'd decorated with Meg on Christmas Eve, but it was only fair for him to spend more time with her now, during the allotted days.

Just as soon as they were both inside.

He donned his hat. "I look forward to our time together. But as of right now, I am going indoors before I freeze. You ought to do the same."

He waited for a moment, but when she appeared to have no notion of moving, he shrugged and turned to the door again. He reached for the handle but gasped when his hat was knocked from his head.

He darted around at the sound of Meg's laughter. "You are asking for trouble," he warned, eying his hat on the landing, covered in snow.

She grinned in response, reaching down for another handful of snow.

"Don't you dare," he said, holding up his arm too late, the snow hitting his shoulder. Her laughter rang out once more. "Very well, Miss Baker. You have awakened the feral badger within me."

She took a step back, turning her body sideways as if preparing to dart away. "Don't you mean a feral mole?"

"You are finished," he said, bolting towards her. Her laughter trailed out behind her as she ran across the snow. "I told you not to criticize my costume."

He slowed his pace for a moment, reaching down to gather a quick handful of snow. He threw it softly as he straightened, but it sailed past her without a touch.

Her chortling sounded all the louder. He attempted to throw another, but she dodged to the right. His coat fell down from around her shoulders, landing with a soft thud in the snow.

"You always were a terrible aim!" Meg shouted over her shoulder.

It was true. She'd always been better at that than him. Although, when she boasted in her abilities, he didn't mind. Unlike Miss Michaels cheating the day before, Meg won honestly.

He chased after her. "Well perhaps I will stop throwing snow at you then and simply throw *you* at the snow."

Their joyful laughter merged as he approached, her quick steps no match for his long stride. In a matter of moments, he caught up with her, reaching out and grasping her wrist. She squealed as his other arm curled around her waist, turning her to face him. His arms wrapped around her, and he brought her closer toward him, lifting her in the air and making a motion to feign throwing her in the snow.

She squirmed, breathless with laughter. "I forfeit. I forfeit!"

With a chuckle, he lowered her feet to the ground, though he kept his arms around her. "You should know better than to provoke me, Meg. I always win."

She stared up at him, her laughter subsiding and smile softening. Her fingers clasped together as she pressed them to her chest. "Always?" she asked, still breathing heavily. "Might I have some hope of winning one day?"

He stared up at the snowflakes still falling, pretending to ponder her question. "Perhaps one day, if you are persistent enough. And if you do not give up so easily as you have done now."

He dropped his eyes to give her a pointed look, but when he noted her serious expression, his teasing smile faded away. The falling snowflakes clung to her blonde locks like dainty pearls. Her face was thinner than he remembered. When had it lost its girlish shape? And when had her cheeks become so rosy, her lips so red?

He'd always thought Meg was pretty, but she was more than that now. Somewhere in the jumble of his being occupied with school and his attempts to keep things the same in his life, he'd missed the change that had occurred. She was not the same girl he'd known before. His friend was now a woman. A beautiful, grown, and accomplished lady who smelled of peppermint.

Their eyes met, the blue of hers like the color of snow blanketing the fields at night. As he perused her face, a small spark lit in his chest. He welcomed the comforting feeling as it warmed his limbs and caused his heart to skip a beat.

But the warmth blew out as swiftly as a single, trembling candle when the door to Hollridge clicked open nearby. Matthew dropped his hands, and he and Meg both took a simultaneous step away from each other as they faced Matthew's father standing in the open doorway.

"Your mother and Louisa have been looking for you both," Father said. He paused, his eyes lingering on Meg's dress before dropping to Matthew's coat strewn across the snow. "You two do know it is snowing out here, do you not?"

Matthew could barely comprehend Father's comment, his mind reeling with confusion. What was that…that warmth that occurred within him as he held his friend in his arms? How had it felt so natural, so right? And why in heaven's name did he feel as if he'd been caught sneaking extra sweets or slipping out of church early?

He fidgeted with his collar, heat rising up his neck. "Yes, Father. That is why we are out here—because of the snow."

Father's eyes moved between the two of them. "Very well. I'll leave you both to your merriment then."

"No need, Mr. Pratt," Meg said, leaving Matthew's side and making for the house. "I am excessively cold now and should like to sit by the fire."

Father smiled warmly at Meg as she walked past him. He turned next to Matthew. "What of you, son?"

"I suppose I will, as well."

He retrieved his coat from the snow, not bothering to place it around his shoulders. He didn't really need it anyway. He was feeling a little overheated.

He approached Father, who held the door open for him. "How are you fairing with your mother's bargain?" his father asked under his breath.

Matthew glanced through the open doorway and around the front hall to ensure Meg was nowhere in sight. "Easier than I ever anticipated," he lied.

Father clapped his hand on Matthew's shoulder. "Excellent. And what of our own wager? I trust you've not fallen in love with anyone yet."

Matthew forced a flippant laugh at his father's teasing. "Of course not. Your task is even easier than Mother's."

He walked away with a forced smirk, ignoring Father's knowing smile and the unsettling heat that returned to his chest at his father's question—and the memory it evoked of Meg's eyes peering into his own.

That night, Meg sat with the Pratts in the drawing room after dinner. With her legs tucked under her on the settee, the glowing fire's warmth extended to all in the room, and Louisa's animated tone reading *The Mysteries of Udolpho*, Meg should have felt a great deal of comfort. These were some of her favorite moments with the Pratts, especially during Christmastide, when they had no parties to attend, no people to call upon. Just the five of them enjoying one another's company.

So why in heaven's name could she not keep her fingers from fidgeting with the lace at the bottom of her dress, or her eyes from repetitively straying to where Matthew sat playing chess with his father?

Of course she already knew the answer, but she wouldn't allow her mind to linger there for long. After all, she was sure that Matthew peering into her eyes as the snow drifted down around them hadn't meant a thing to him, though it had to her. As he'd held her in his arms, she had almost revealed her true feelings. Had Matthew discovered them? Had she scared him away?

Louisa paused in her reading, stifling a yawn behind her fingers.

"Are you to stop for the night, my dear?" Mrs. Pratt asked, sitting on a chair nearest the fire.

Louisa shook her head. "When I'm finished with this chapter. Unless anyone has objection to my continuing?"

She glanced about the room then smiled happily to herself at the general consensus for her to carry on.

As she took up the story once more, Meg caught Mrs. Pratt's eye. She returned her kind smile then looked away.

She'd always loved the woman. The Pratts had only lived in Haxby for a few weeks before her parents had dropped Meg off on their doorstep for the first time. Apparently, the Bakers preferred her to be in the care of the Pratts, as opposed to just her governess, as they had done for prior years.

At first, Meg had been terrified to be near the towering Mrs. Pratt, but in a matter of days, she came to see just how wonderfully different she was from her own mother. She took her dress shopping, listened to her sorrows, always treated her with kindness. Meg loved her, and she thought Mrs. Pratt returned that love.

So why was she pushing seemingly every other woman—apart from Meg—toward Matthew? Was Meg so very unlikeable? Did Mrs. Pratt not wish Meg to be a part of their permanent family?

The doubting questions assailed her mind until a movement caught her eye, and Mrs. Pratt moved to sit down beside her on the settee.

Meg pulled in her feet with a smile, though her eyes skirted away.

"How are you this evening, dear Meg?" Mrs. Pratt whispered, using the endearment each of the Pratts had adopted for years.

She spoke softly enough to not interrupt Louisa's reading,

though Louisa was staring at the pages so intently, Meg was certain nothing could break her concentration.

"I am well," Meg responded, hoping her words sounded more convincing than they felt to her heart.

"Are you certain? You seem a little, well, a little troubled."

Mrs. Pratt had always been able to discern her feelings. When Meg had attended her first ball, she sat out three dances in a row, and her young self could hardly handle the embarrassment. While Meg's parents sampled the refreshments, Mrs. Pratt had brought Matthew forward from his hiding place near the edge of the ballroom to dance with Meg. Afterward, she'd had a partner for every dance, something she knew she had to attribute to Mrs. Pratt's persuasive words.

With how astute the woman was, Meg attempting to hide her feelings would be futile. Still, she couldn't admit to loving Matthew. Not while she was still unsure as to why Mrs. Pratt didn't love Meg enough to want her as part of the Pratt family.

In response, she simply shrugged.

Mrs. Pratt reached over, squeezing Meg's hand with her own. "I understand perfectly, my dear. I will press you no further. Merely know that I am here to help, should you ever be in need of it. I wish for your happiness, as I do for all my children."

The words struck Meg as realization finally took hold of her mind. Mrs. Pratt wanted Meg and Matthew to both be happy. That was why she wasn't pushing for Meg to be his spouse—because she had no idea Meg was in love with her son.

Shame gripped its frigid fingers around Meg's heart. Mrs. Pratt loved her, perhaps even more than her own mother did. How could she have ever thought otherwise?

"Thank you, Mrs. Pratt," she whispered.

A look of sympathy crossed Mrs. Pratt's features so keenly, Meg instantly had to fight back tears.

"I...I know it cannot be easy with your parents away so often," Mrs. Pratt said, "nor is it easy when they are here. But I must tell you, last year was very hard on us while you were at Stoneworth. There was a distinctively sweet spirit missing from our home that could only be filled with your presence. How glad we all are that you are here celebrating with us again this winter."

Unable to say a word but wishing to express her love and gratitude for the woman who had brought such happiness to her life, Meg merely smiled. Mrs. Pratt, seeming to understand, patted Meg's hand once more then leaned back on the settee, remaining at Meg's side as she returned her focus to Louisa, who hadn't missed a beat in her reading.

Meg tried to pay attention to the words, but her thoughts continued to run. A fleeting desire to tell Mrs. Pratt the truth flickered in her mind, but she disregarded it. If all of the Pratts knew of her feelings, and Matthew ended up refusing her, she couldn't bear the embarrassment, nor the compassion, that would surely follow. The rejection would be far easier to bear with only Louisa aware.

But Matthew wouldn't reject her. Would he?

Her eyes made their way across the room to where he sat at the chess table. Instead of his attention being focused on the pieces of his game, it was directed toward Meg. Her stomach flipped, settling down with a firm thud. She sent him a hesitant smile when he maintained his staring, but he made no move to return it, nor did he blink, staring at her in an obvious daze.

"You do realize it is your turn, Matthew?" Mr. Pratt whispered.

Matthew blinked, pulling his eyes from Meg. "Yes, merely thinking."

Meg watched him for only a moment longer, but he did not look her way again. Instead his attention moved from the game to his sister, whom he watched with soft eyes and clear, brotherly affection. Was that not the same way he'd been staring at Meg?

The logs settled farther into the fireplace, and she turned her attention to the embers shooting above the blaze, the flames brightening for a moment before dying down, just like her hope of Matthew ever seeing her as more than his sister.

CHAPTER 6

"*A*re we all looking forward to the evening?"

Meg eyed Mrs. Pratt, who sat across from her in the carriage. The woman was obviously seeking positivity from her family and Meg, but hardly anyone could manage to muster more than a weak smile in response.

"Of course, my dear," Mr. Pratt responded, though his own light tone didn't reach his eyes. "We always enjoy a party at the Warrens'."

Yes. They enjoyed a party at the Warrens' as greatly as one would enjoy the removal of a frostbitten toe.

Meg stared out of the window at the patches of snow that remained scattered across the dark, frozen countryside. The Warrens were a kind enough family, but their affluence made their two single daughters rather unbearable. This New Year's Eve, Meg didn't have the energy nor the patience to handle such snobbery. Not when all she wanted was to relive the three previous days she'd spent with Matthew.

She glanced sidelong at him. His head and shoulders moved back and forth as the carriage bounced along the roadway. He had certainly kept up his end of the bargain the last few days, as he always did with the deals he made. He'd spent every moment from morning to evening with Meg and Louisa, buying sweets for them at the bakery, enjoying horse rides together, and playing games until well into the night. This made it all the more difficult to look forward to an evening of sharing him with the Warrens.

As the carriage stopped in front of Casterly Hall, Meg exited and moved her eyes about the grand house with its matching curved stairways, and four towering columns lining up to reach the double doors. It certainly was garish. Perfect for the Warrens.

"Are you ready to entertain tonight, Matthew?" she asked as they walked together side by side up the steps.

"Not by any means. But am I ever?"

His light words were void of any teasing smile. She felt for him. The man truly despised socializing. "Well, not to worry. I shall make this evening enjoyable for you."

"And how do you plan on doing that?"

"I have my ways."

She sent him a coy look, to which he finally responded with a smile of his own.

Matthew had always been the one to improve Meg's mood when they were children. When she'd first arrived at Hollridge, she'd hardly said a word to anyone. She wasn't listened to by her parents, so why would the Pratts treat her any differently? It was Matthew, however, who had finally been able to pull her from her voiceless hiding place with his friendly teasing and kind attention.

Not much had changed. Except, of course, her feelings for him.

They entered the house and moved with the footman to the drawing room where they were greeted at once by the warmth of the fire, the smell of steaming tea and sweet foods, and the sounds of laughter and conversation as more than twenty people filled the spacious room.

Multiple tables were set up, adorned with bright candles and new decks of cards. A refreshment area was arranged at the back of the room. Covering the table were crystal glasses for port and sherry and shining silver trays heaping with pastries, cold meats, and various finger foods, ready for guests to serve themselves when hungry or parched.

The greenery decking the drawing room made Hollridge House feel scant and bare. Every window was brightened with tapers in gold and glass candleholders. The mantelpiece flourished with foliage, and each table around the room was decorated with twigs of berries tied together with ribbons and placed on top of an evergreen bough.

Even with all the lavishness, Meg preferred the comfort and relaxed, unassuming atmosphere of the Pratts' home.

"So happy you could join us this evening," Mrs. Warren said, approaching the Pratts and Meg as Mr. Warren and their daughters trailed closely behind.

"Mr. Matthew Pratt," Mr. Warren said. "You remember our youngest, Miss Josephine."

"Yes, indeed," Matthew responded. He bowed to the girl, and she responded with a graceful curtsy, her dark ringlets bouncing happily at her temples.

Miss Josephine and her older sister, Miss Warren, exchanged identical smiles. Meg cringed. The Warrens' wealth was no secret, nor was the desire of the daughters to wed wealthy and attractive gentlemen. They would never settle for anyone who couldn't support or approve of their affluent living—like Matthew—but that never stopped them from flirting with gentlemen who caught their fancy for the evening.

"We have been looking forward to this party for quite some time," Mrs. Pratt said, the only one of them who seemed to be speaking the truth. "We haven't enjoyed a night of games for many months."

Mrs. Warren shook her head, her emerald earrings swinging back and forth. "Oh, neither have we. Although, I must say, this party almost did not occur."

She paused heavily, baiting them for a story.

Meg did not care to discover what Mrs. Warren wished to boast of now, but Mrs. Pratt kindly indulged.

"Why ever not?"

Mrs. Warren exchanged proud glances with her husband. "Only a few days ago, we received an invitation to attend a dinner party by Miss June Rosewall herself."

Meg stifled a yawn, looking about the room and longing to visit with the other guests, if only to escape the tiresome gossip. She'd heard of June Rosewall, of course, the elderly, never-married woman who kept only to herself and her close friends. Miss Rosewall had no family, as far as Meg was aware, though she'd heard rumors of an estranged nephew in Cornwall. The woman was rather bad-tempered, but she was wealthy and regal, so many families wished to be honored with an invitation to become more acquainted with her.

As Mrs. Warren continued on about how Miss Rosewall promised another invitation, Meg glanced to Miss Josephine, who still stared unabashedly at Matthew.

Meg hadn't spent a great deal of time around Miss Josephine, as the girl had only been introduced into Society this last Season at sixteen, but what Meg had observed was that Miss Josephine was even more of a flirt than her older sister.

"Mr. Pratt," the girl said interrupting her mother, who merely turned doting eyes on her daughter, "I understand you've not been to Casterly Hall in over a year. Might I take you on a tour of our drawing room?"

Matthew gave her a humored look, but Miss Josephine raised her dainty eyebrows in a question. "Oh," he said, sobering at once. "Yes, I would enjoy that."

He must have thought her offer to tour around a single room—though spacious as it was—was a joke. Meg had thought so as well.

The two of them moved away from the others to walk about the room as Miss Warren, Louisa, and Meg stared after them. Frustration festered within Meg. She didn't like the idea of someone flirting with Matthew purely for pleasure. Of course, she didn't like the idea of someone flirting with him for any reason at all, especially Miss Josephine. If she had convinced her parents to let her out in Society before her sister was married, what else was she capable of doing?

As Meg tried to keep her attention from wavering to the two of them, the final guests arrived and the games began. A number of couples moved to the card tables, starting games of whist, hazard, and loo, as a few of the guests remained by the hearth, wishing to speak instead of play.

The rest of the party made their way to the far side of the room where green-cushioned chairs were arranged in a large circle. The guests sat down alternately between lady and gentleman. Matthew took a seat next to Meg, her heart as warm as the wassail they'd shared the night before. Louisa moved to sit beside her brother, but Miss Josephine slipped in at the last moment.

"Oh, you don't mind if I sit here, do you, Miss Pratt? After all, you are able to see your brother for as long as you wish while at home. We, however, see so very little of him." Her eyes sparkled as she glanced to Matthew.

Matthew sent an apologetic look to Louisa, who walked to an empty seat across the circle next to Mr. Richards, a young gentleman with a deep dimple in his chin. Meg knew it was difficult for Louisa to be parted from her twin while he was at university, even more so than it was for Meg. Miss Josephine, of course, didn't know such a thing, nor would she care if she did.

Meg fought the desire to stand up and pull the chair right out from under the girl. Instead, she caught Louisa's attention and motioned to her own seat.

"Do you wish to sit here?" she mouthed.

Louisa shook her head with a wave of her hand. Before Meg could insist, Miss Warren clapped her hands, her gloves causing a soft thud as she caught the attention of the others. "Shall we begin with a game of short answers?"

The group agreed, and she set about explaining the rules to ensure they were all in accord. "Only a one-syllable word may be responded to each question, and no answers or questions may be repeated. Those who falter shall be removed from the game until another round ensues or a different game begins. Agreed?" The group nodded before she turned to Mr. Richards who sat at her right and Louisa's left. "Now, Mr. Richards, I shall begin. Do tell me, do you enjoy reading?"

Mr. Richards appeared to think a great deal before he responded with, "No." Then he looked around the room for nods of appreciation for his clever response.

When he said nothing further, Miss Warren nodded. "Now you must ask Miss Pratt a question, sir."

"Ah, of course." He turned to Louisa. "Pray, Miss Pratt, what is your favorite color?"

"Green."

"Ah, excellent, I thought I'd capture you there for certain."

Louisa politely smiled before exchanging glances with Meg. They'd often joked about Mr. Richards's simplicity. He was a good sort of man, though, respectful and courteous, so they tried not to speak too critically of him.

The game continued until the gentleman at Meg's left, Mr. Barton, turned his eyes on Meg. His wife had obviously coerced him into playing, as he sat leaning far back in his chair with his arms folded and a grim stretch to his lips. "What county boasts the most spectacular coastline?"

Meg thought for a moment. She knew Cornwall was her first choice. She'd spent a summer there as a child with the Pratts, and she and the twins had spent hours searching for seashells in the sand and playing in the sea water. But with only a one-syllable word allowed, it would have to be, "Kent."

A murmur of assent trailed around her before she turned to Matthew. "Don't make this too hard on me," he said softly.

She smiled up at him. "What animal were you dressed as for the masquerade in London?"

His jaw twitched, and he stared at her with feigned annoyance. Her innocent smile continued, though joy ignited in her heart. If he spoke truthfully, a badger, then he'd lose the game. But if he answered with one syllable…

Finally, in a flat tone, he said, "Mole."

She gleefully laughed, though the others in the circle exchanged confused glances, unaware of their little joke. "As I suspected all along. A mole with a stained underbelly."

He stifled a laugh before turning to Miss Josephine. "May I ask how you prefer your tea, miss?"

Miss Josephine tapped her forefinger against her chin before sticking it straight up in the air. "Hot!" she exclaimed before laughing at her own excitement.

"Excellent," Matthew responded. "A very clever response, indeed."

Clever? Meg's smile faded. The answer was not so very clever. Meg was certain she could conjure multiple responses to such a question. Nothing that she could come up with now, of course, but that hardly mattered.

Miss Josephine faced the gentleman next to her with the question, "What is the season in which we are experiencing now?" which resulted in the man's expulsion after he replied with "Winter."

Soon, Miss Warren redirected the questions to go the opposite way, and in a matter of moments, Miss Josephine's turn came again. She faced Matthew directly with a flirtatious smile. "Are you ready, sir?"

"Yes," he replied. Then he turned away, clapping his hands on his thighs with a happy grin. "Well, that was no doubt the easiest question I've answered playing this game."

The group laughed, Miss Josephine the loudest. Meg's toes curled in her slippers.

"No, Mr. Pratt," Miss Josephine said, "that was not my question, you tease! No, here is my *real* question. What color do you prefer your steeds to be?"

Matthew responded with a genuine smile. Of course he would smile. The question was about a horse. "Black," he responded.

He looked to Meg, but Miss Josephine continued. "Oh, excellent choice, sir. I do love black horses the very best."

"Do you ride?" he asked.

"As often as I can. There is no greater pleasure, nor no greater animal."

Meg shifted in her seat. Either Miss Josephine was an exceptional liar, or she really did enjoy horses as equally as Matthew.

The girl continued, tipping her head so her ringlets bobbed in the air like small, curled ribbons. "I'm sure you agree with me. I am well aware of your love for the animal."

"How do you know such a thing?"

"Everyone knows such a thing, Matthew," Louisa piped up across the circle. "We all know you prefer the animal to anyone else, humans included."

The group laughed, and Matthew and his sister exchanged smiles. Miss Warren cleared her throat. "Mr. Pratt, I believe it is your turn to ask a question."

"Of course."

The game continued. Matthew seemed in a far more jovial mood, making teasing comments and laughing as the group did. But was this because of the game or because Miss Josephine was far more entertaining than Meg? That girl was quickly being added to Meg's acquaintance list.

Mr. Richards was the next to be removed after he'd responded to his favorite pastime as "reading." Miss Warren followed soon after, much to her chagrin, after she'd replied, "No," to a question.

"I'm quite certain that answer has not been given yet," she said, her nose pointed to the ceiling, shoulders as straight as the back of her chair.

"I'm sorry, my dear sister, but it most assuredly has by Mr. Richards," Miss Josephine said with a giggle.

Miss Warren moved away from the group with a flutter of skirts, muttering, "I'm happy to be finished with this game. I hardly enjoy it."

Miss Josephine giggled at her sister's unceremonious departure.

As the players were whittled down, the questions became more difficult, and the answers even more so.

Excepting, of course, any question Miss Josephine asked Matthew, all of which were related to horses. She was clearly attempting to draw Matthew's good favor, but much to Meg's aversion, it appeared to be working. Matthew continued to strike up conversations with the girl about what breed of horse she rode and when she took up riding.

Meg could hardly stand listening to the two of them speak. Nor, did it seem, could Louisa. When asked by Mr. Billings how she felt that evening, she replied, "Very well." Then immediately stood from her seat with a blank expression. "Oh, dear. It appears I have lost."

Miss Josephine nodded goodbye to Louisa, who promptly left the circle without a glance in the girl's direction.

When Mr. Billings was expelled from the game next, Meg was left alone with Matthew and Miss Josephine. She rolled her shoulders to dispel the tension rising in her muscles, tension caused by the girl's next question spoken in her high-pitched voice.

"Pray, Mr. Pratt, what is a pretty young woman to do to be noticed by a handsome gentleman?"

Matthew hardly seemed aware of her brazen question, responding simply with, "Breathe."

He laughed at his own joke before facing Meg. She forced a smile, though her heart felt as empty as the seats now surrounding them. Miss Josephine was pursuing Matthew that evening for only a bit of fun, and Matthew didn't seem to mind the attention at all.

"Where might you find the River Thames?" he asked.

Meg would have replied swiftly with Town, but she held her tongue. Did she truly wish to be around Miss Josephine any longer, fawning over the love of her life?

"London," she said with a sigh, hoping to feign losing better than Louisa had.

"Oh, Miss Baker," Miss Josephine cried out, "you have been bested at last! And with such a simple question. My first answer would have been Town, you know."

"I had not even thought of such a response," Meg said, rising from her seat and ignoring Matthew's suspicious expression. "Well done, Miss Josephine."

She walked away, and the girl's words drifted towards her. "Now, Mr. Pratt, it is down to the both of us, the wittiest in the room."

Meg found Louisa near the table of food. She walked up to her, retrieving a small plate and eying the pastries as Matthew responded to yet another question about a horse.

"I take it you answered incorrectly on purpose, as well?" Louisa asked Meg in a soft tone, taking a rather large bite of a mince pie.

"How did you know?" Meg asked with a scoff, placing one piece of cheesecake on her plate before making it two. She needed that extra sweetness to improve her mood tonight.

"She is certainly doing her best to draw attention to herself, isn't she?" Louisa asked. "I thought her sister was bad, but Miss Warren is a saint compared to Miss Josephine."

The girl responded to another of Matthew's questions, and he threw back his head with laughter. An ache trailed down Meg's chest, as if the cheesecake she'd just swallowed had turned to stone.

"I do wonder if Matthew can see through her behavior," Meg said with half-hope, half-fear.

"I'm sure he can. I only…" Louisa's eyes flitted over Meg's shoulder, and a false smile appeared on her lips. "Miss Warren, there you are."

Meg turned around as Miss Warren approached them. "I trust you find the food to your liking, ladies."

"Indeed," Louisa said. "As delicious as always."

Meg pretended to chew her bite of cheesecake so she wouldn't have to speak.

Louisa continued. "It was good of your parents to not cancel the party this evening, despite the prestigious invitation they received."

Miss Warren idly spun her golden ring round her fifth and smallest finger. "Yes, but I cannot understand their logic, putting the people of Haxby, of all places, above a woman like Miss Rosewall. Then again, my parents are not known for their sense, are they?"

Meg's lips fell at her words. How could Miss Warren speak of her parents in such a way? What Meg wouldn't give for parents like the Warrens. Doting, attentive, present—everything that her parents weren't. She'd never had anyone constant in her life like that, apart from the Pratts.

She glanced toward him, forcing herself to keep a level head, though Matthew's smile grew as he spoke with the girl.

"They seem to be quite taken with their game, do they not?" Miss Warren said, also watching her sister with a focused stare. "Or, perhaps, taken with each other."

She sent a knowing look to Louisa before walking away without another word.

Matthew could not be taken with Miss Josephine. She was too young. Too wealthy. Too sure of herself. Too...not Meg.

She glanced to Louisa, who had turned a slightly ashen color. "Are you well?"

Louisa looked up from her plate. "Hmm? Oh, indeed. I...I'm merely feeling a little full."

She left her plate on the table then crossed the room with a hand pressed to her stomach. Meg looked after her, wondering at her behavior, before facing Matthew once again.

After a quarter of an hour, the game was won by Miss Josephine, who was not shy to boast her accomplishment to the rest of the party.

The evening progressed with more games and food, but Meg's spirits steadily declined as she tried and failed to ignore Matthew's laughter at Miss Josephine's comments. She'd never seen him laugh so much with anyone but herself, and the knowledge was crushing.

Finally, as the end of the night neared, the large party gathered in the front hall, circling together as they anxiously awaited the midnight hour. Meg forced herself to cheer along with the others as twelve o'clock arrived, and Mr. Warren ran to open the front door, ushering in the new year.

Next, he moved through the house, the large party following behind him as they headed to one of the back doors where they would symbolically let the old year pass through. Meg typically enjoyed the tradition, but as she brought up the rear of the group alone, she longed for the evening to end.

A draft rushed past her, and she shivered, folding her arms. Was she chilled because of cold corridor? Or was it because Matthew still laughed with Miss Josephine at the front of the line? Either way, she would use the excuse to return to the drawing room for her wrap. A little space from that shrill laughter would do her much good.

Silently, she turned around. What a terrible night this was. Matthew unable to keep away from the Warrens, Louisa remaining silent the rest of the evening. Her friends' behavior and Meg's forlorn spirits had made for a very depressing New Year's Eve, indeed.

When she reached the drawing room, the warmth of the large fire instantly soothed her, and she was tempted to linger in the room. But when she caught sight of the green chairs they sat upon for their game, memories of Miss Josephine's high-pitched tone grated on the last of her nerves.

She retrieved her shawl and Louisa's—knowing her friend would be near frozen if Meg was slightly chilled—grumbling as she did so.

"Oh, I love horses, Mr. Pratt," she murmured in a high falsetto voice, imitating Miss Josephine as she threw her shawl round her shoulders. "They are so perfect and beautiful. Just like I am. Do you not love my hair and my perfect posture and my dress and—"

"They are rather nice."

Meg gasped, whirling around to find Matthew leaning against the doorframe with folded arms, an amused smile playing on his lips.

"But typically, you do not require such praise from me," he finished.

Her cheeks burned. "Matthew. How-how long were you standing there?"

He pushed himself away from the doorframe and walked into the room. "Long enough to know who you mimicked. I must say, I'm impressed. I did not know your voice could reach quite so high."

Meg shifted her gaze. She needed to change the subject before he asked *why* she'd been mimicking Miss Josephine. "Why are you not with the others?"

"Mother sent me to retrieve Louisa's wrap," he said, motioning to the shawl in Meg's hand, "but I see you have beaten me to it. Now, tell me, why were you imitating Miss Josephine so skillfully?"

Blast. "No reason." He dropped his chin with a dubious expression, but she rushed on, desperate to turn the attention on him. "You seem to have been enjoying your evening with her though."

"I suppose. She is an entertaining young lady, but she is a worse flirt than her sister was at her age. Though Miss Warren seems to have grown out of it."

Hope pushed past the coldness in her heart like a hellebore flower breaking through the snow. Still, she forced herself to remain flippant. "So she didn't capture you with all her talk of horses then?"

He scoffed. "She certainly thought she knew a great deal about them. Do you know, she actually tried telling me I was wrong about the breed of my own horse? You and Louisa know far more than she does. I eventually ignored her errors and just responded with laughter."

Meg couldn't hide her smile. She should've known Miss Josephine would slip up eventually. If there was one thing the man couldn't be corrected on, it would be his knowledge of horses.

"Why are you smiling?" he asked before wincing. "You and Louisa haven't assumed I've taken a liking to the girl, have you?"

Meg could have laughed. They absolutely *had* thought that, just like they had with Miss Paulson. However, his happy manner with Miss Josephine—as opposed to his rather reserved behavior with Miss Paulson—had almost convinced Meg that his mother had found someone for him to love at last. How relieved she was that it was not true, yet again.

"Honestly," he said, rubbing the back of his neck, "I cannot believe the sheer amount of women the two of you have wished for me to marry."

Actually, Meg knew of only one.

Matthew joined Meg as they crossed the room.

"Can you blame us?" she asked. "We've never known you to speak to so many women in your life."

He paused in the doorway. She was right to be suspicious. He had spent more time with more women than he'd ever had before, including women he would never choose to converse with, like the Warrens. During the brief moments he'd been able to pry away from Miss Josephine, he'd managed a few words with her sister, but he was clearly the last gentleman Miss Warren wished to speak with that evening.

Still, he'd tried, and with the evening nearing its end and numbers five and six seen to, he could almost taste the freedom of riding on his new horse, no longer needing to return to Mother for yet another lecture on why he needed to marry and help Father with the estate.

Now if only he could tell Meg his reasoning. But then, he was so close to completing his task. He'd come too far to give up now. He would simply have to create better ways to hide the bargains from now on.

"Well, perhaps I have simply changed while at university," he said. "Perhaps I have felt the need to be more kind to others."

Meg snorted, a sound deemed improper for most women, though it only endeared him to his friend more.

"You don't believe me?"

"Not in the slightest," she said. "But it doesn't matter. I have my own secrets I am unwilling to divulge."

"Do you now?"

She nodded.

"And what secrets, pray tell, are those?"

"No, no, Mr. Pratt. We are no longer playing a game. I don't have to answer that now."

They shared a smile. He'd missed their repartee today. The past few days he'd spent with her and Louisa had been wonderful, once he'd gotten rid of whatever feeling he'd had that moment they'd shared in the snow. Since then, it hadn't returned, so he'd simply chalked it up to indigestion or the simple joy that came from knowing he'd won their snow fight.

He'd wanted to spend more time with her at the party, as well, but with the bargain in place with two women that evening—and Miss Josephine attaching herself to him like a piece of lint—he'd hardly had a moment to do so. He was sorely tempted to hide away in the drawing room with Meg until the carriages were ready, but his sister needed her shawl.

"Shall we return to the others then?" he asked.

Meg hesitated. "Yes, I suppose so. Only, may I keep you here for just a moment longer? I wish to express my gratitude to you for these past few days, for seeing through with your promise and spending time with me and Louisa. I have to admit, we highly enjoyed ourselves."

His heart warmed. Meg had never hesitated to express her gratitude to him and his family, even for the simplest of acts. He supposed her grateful nature was born from having worthless parents. He pressed down his anger—simmering at the mere thought of the Bakers—with mischief. "You know me, Meg. I would never say no to more time of leisure."

"Or to a bargain?"

"You really have no idea."

She studied him for a moment without saying a word.

"What?" he asked as her silence continued, unnerving him.

"I'm merely attempting to conjure a deal with which you would be unable to agree."

He chuckled. "I wish you luck. There never has been such a one."

"Really?"

"Absolutely."

"Very well, then I have one for you now." Her eyes shone brightly, the candlelight from the sconces in the corridor reflecting in their blue depths. "If you accept my challenge, I agree to take the blame when next we are in Society and you wish for a bit of respite in a darkened corridor."

Instantly, he shook his head. "We have already attempted that at the masquerade, if you recall. Mother still blamed our absence on me."

"No, no. I promise, I will not accept anything less than the total amount of the responsibility."

Matthew thought for a moment before nodding. "Very well, I can agree to that. Now what would you have *me* do?"

Her lips curved. "I would have you kiss me."

CHAPTER 7

$\mathcal{M}$atthew pulled back, his brow low over his eyes. "You…what?"

"I trust you heard me so I do not have to repeat myself," Meg said, her voice smooth as she raised a determined chin.

He felt for the doorframe behind him, resting his hand against the wood. He was only vaguely aware of his palms beginning to sweat. "But why?"

She released a tiresome sigh. "I am standing beneath a kissing bough, Matthew Pratt. Why else would I ask for such a thing?"

He leaned back, catching sight of the ball of mistletoe and greenery hanging above them in a circle, tied together with a neat, red bow. A strange feeling came over him. Disappointment? Relief? He couldn't be sure.

"Oh, of course. Well that's an easy task then isn't it?"

He shook away the nerves that had crept into his shoulders. He'd kissed Meg before beneath a kissing bough. He could do it again.

He leaned forward and placed a quick peck to her cheek. It was over before it had even begun. "There. Now, about your end of the bargain. I think if I—"

"Is that all?"

He eyed her frown. "What do you mean?"

"Is that all I receive for my end of the bargain?"

He hesitated. Why was she so disappointed? That is how they had kissed every year beneath the mistletoe. "I-I didn't think you'd wish for anything more."

She huffed. "Do you not think I *deserve* more for the deal we have struck? After all, I'm going to make your mother very upset with me. Perhaps she throws me from Hollridge House, what then? And all for a simple kiss you would bestow upon your grandmother?"

He could see her point, but an anxiousness settled across him, and he wrung his hands. Was she asking for…He shook the thought from his mind. "Very well. A kiss to your brow then?"

She gave him a dull look—lowering her brow, half-hooding her eyes—then faced him squarely. Silently, she tapped a forefinger against her lips.

He'd expected that she'd been hinting such an action. After all, a kiss on the lips *was* greater than bestowing one on the cheek or forehead. Still, his heart quickened.

"You…you wish for a real kiss?" he asked, wondering why, after all these years, she would wish for one now.

She shrugged. "It is not so strange, Matthew. I've seen countless others do so beneath the mistletoe." She straightened and raised her chin. "Come now, no more dawdling."

It was true then, Meg wanted him to kiss her. But why? What would that prove? And more importantly, did he wish to kiss her in return?

Blood rushed throughout him, burning the tips of his ears. He stared down at her, her shining blue eyes watching him, her red lips parted and ready to share in his affection. His heart beat so heavily against his chest, it felt bruised.

Was he really going to do this? Was he going to kiss his friend?
His friend.

He clenched his teeth together, muffling his thoughts with an imaginary cover. It didn't matter what he desired. Meg was his friend, and he didn't wish to ruin that.

He glanced over his shoulder to keep from staring at the moisture glinting on Meg's lips. "What if we are discovered by the others or the servants?"

"The servants will be celebrating downstairs still, and the party, I'm certain, will have barely arrived at the back door by now." Meg sighed, returning his attention to her as she placed her hands on her hips. "Honestly, Matthew, it is only a simple kiss. And we *are* standing under the kissing bough, you remember. No one would think twice about seeing such a thing."

No one, except perhaps Mother. She *had* instructed Matthew not to kiss any of the nine. Though, did Meg really count towards the list? A kiss might make things awkward between them, but was it possible that he was simply overthinking the whole issue?

"I'm not sure about this, Meg," he said, rubbing the back of his neck.

She stared at him wide-eyed. "I never thought I'd see the day that *you* would say no to a bargain."

She was goading him. He knew that. But blast if it wasn't working. He felt the itch to win, to accept her deal and succeed, but he couldn't scratch it. Could he?

"A bargain, I might add, that is well in your favor," Meg continued.

Matthew tapped his foot on the threshold. Very well, a simple, holiday kiss could not ruin their friendship of more than ten years. After all, many people participated in the amusement. Why couldn't they?

"If it is too much for you to handle, Matthew, I understand. You needn't accept my offer for the first time in your life."

He really should swallow his pride, ignore his need to win every challenge put before him. But he needed to keep his record strong. And that adorably charming smirk needed to be wiped from Meg's face once and for all.

She raised a flippant shoulder. "I suppose I'll have to tell—"

He reached forward with one hand, ending her words as he

slipped his fingers around the back of her neck and placed his lips on hers.

He intended for the kiss to only last a moment, long enough to stop her goading and put his pride above her own. But when he acknowledged the warmth of her lips, that strange feeling from before blossomed in his chest. Heat spread throughout him, as if he'd just had a steaming cup of chocolate. Only, Meg's lips tasted of peppermint.

When they were younger, Matthew had occasionally wondered how it would be to kiss Meg, though he'd always set the thought aside, thinking it would be strange to kiss his friend. However, with her gentle lips on his, softer than he ever could have imagined, the action felt natural, perfect. As if they had been sharing in this affection for the entirety of their lives.

The fire crackled in the hearth behind them, the only sound reaching his ears apart from their soft, slow breaths. He stroked the back of her neck with his fingertips. He should have removed his gloves before this. How he longed to feel the smoothness of her skin.

The warmth strengthened, stirring and awakening indiscernible feelings deep inside, and his heart took flight, thudding mutely in his ears before he was lost.

Meg didn't move, though she longed to wrap her arms around Matthew's neck, drink in more of his tender kiss. She was too afraid if she did, the spell would be broken. For this had to be a spell. Magic or sorcery of some sort. Or perhaps it was a miracle? How else could Matthew be kissing her, his lips lingering on hers, his fingers caressing the back of her neck?

How she had dreamt of this moment. How she had longed for it for months. And now, Matthew was kissing her. *Her*, Meg Baker. And—dare she hope?—he was enjoying it.

He tipped his head to the side, his nose pressing softly against her cheek, his breath tickling her skin. She couldn't help herself any longer, she had to touch him.

Slowly, she raised a hand between them, feeling her way up his waistcoat, jacket lapel, cravat, then finally, her gloved fingertips brushed against his jaw. She reached slightly higher until her hand rested at the side of his neck. Her breathing shallowed as she felt his quickened pulse.

He *was* enjoying this.

The knowledge sent her mind spinning. She reached her other hand to grasp his arm, but the deepest regret struck her as their reverie ended, and Matthew pulled back with a start. He stared down at her with rounded eyes, and she held her breath, praying she appeared unaffected by his lips on hers, and their sudden departure.

He dropped his hand and bumped into the doorframe as he took a step back. "Well, there you have it. Will that suffice?"

"Of course." She swallowed. "And I will see to my end of the bargain the moment you wish it."

He pumped his head up and down, his eyes darting away from hers to the kissing bough above. He reached forward, his musky cologne wafting toward her as he plucked a white berry from the bough—fulfilling the custom one shared when kissing beneath it.

"Here," he said, dropping it into her outstretched palm without touching her hand.

Meg nodded with gratitude. His eyes dropped to hers, flitting to her lips for a brief moment before he took a step back and made his way down the corridor.

"We'd better return before they think we've become lost," he said over his shoulder.

Meg watched him practically bound down the corridor without her. She followed after him more slowly, reliving the moment she'd just shared with Matthew over and over again, all the while clutching that little white berry as if it was the most precious pearl in existence.

Because to her, it was.

Matthew had remained hidden away from Meg after their kiss, and she did not see him until they left for the theatre the night after.

Meg had anticipated a level of uncertainty from Matthew. After all, even *she* felt some hesitancy with how to behave around her friend. What she did not expect, however, was for Matthew to completely ignore her, so much as to not even meet her eye.

She attempted again and again to engage him in conversation on their way to York, wishing to show him they could still be friends, to prove to him that nothing had really changed between them, but he only responded with skirted eyes and single-worded answers.

She told herself she was imagining his avoidance of her, but when they reached the theatre, seating themselves with the Wells family in their rented box for the evening, Matthew shuffled swiftly past the others to sit between Miss Wells and Louisa, with no chance of being near Meg.

She took her seat beside Louisa, trying to look to her for comfort, wondering if perhaps her friend might offer to switch her places, but Louisa focused intently on the program in her hands. She must not be feeling herself. She'd been silent all day and looked rather pale. Perhaps she was coming down with a cold.

As they waited for the performance to begin, Matthew's questions to Miss Miles continually drifted toward Meg, but Miss Wells was hardly able to answer. She was a pretty girl with curly, auburn hair, but her timidity resembled a trembling kitten, and her voice was softer than the coo of a turtle dove. Matthew had never spoken highly of her, always commenting on her exhaustive shyness, but that evening, he was clearly more interested in being with her than with Meg, and that whispered to Meg the one thing she didn't wish to believe—that Matthew regretted their kiss.

"Miss Pratt?"

Meg's depressing thoughts ceased, and all eyes turned in their box to a tall man with a wide set of shoulders, standing right before Meg's row.

"Mr. Abbott?" squeaked Louisa.

The squirrel from the masquerade? What was he doing here?

Meg turned swift eyes to Louisa, who's cheeks beamed redder than her rouge.

Louisa stood, giving a slight curtsy with a quick look to her parents. "What a surprise it is to see you here this evening."

"It is a surprise for me, as well, to be seeing you," he said. "I spotted you from across the room and thought to extend my greetings to you and your family."

As he nodded his head to the Pratts, Louisa's eyes darted to Meg's. She was clearly pleading for help to be rid of the gentleman, so Meg stood with a curtsy of her own.

"Whatever are you doing in York, sir?" she asked. "I recall you mentioning you live in Norfolk."

"Yes, but I'm here visiting an old school friend. He and his family are seated just beyond there."

He motioned over his large shoulders. He looked rather more like a bull than a squirrel, especially with that focused, determined gaze on Louisa.

Meg didn't believe his words for a moment. He may be visiting friends, but he'd come to York for clearly one purpose—and that was to find Louisa.

Well, Meg wouldn't stand for her friend to be coerced into spending time with him, as Louisa had been forced to do in London. If she couldn't speak up, Meg would for her.

Before she could kindly remind the gentleman to return to his seat before the performance began, however, Mr. Pratt spoke behind them.

"How long do you plan to stay in York, Mr. Abbott?"

"For a few more weeks, I believe."

"You must join us at Hollridge House for our Twelfth Night revels then," Mrs. Pratt offered.

Meg glanced to Louisa. Could Mrs. Pratt not see her daughter's blush burning brighter? Her shifting eyes? Or was she attempting to push gentlemen toward Louisa as she pushed ladies toward Matthew?

"Thank you, I would enjoy that." Mr. Abbott's smile lingered on Louisa before voices sounded below, signaling the beginning of the performance. "Well, it was a pleasure to see you all again, but I fear I must return to my friends. Good evening."

He tipped forward in a bow then finally broke his concentration on Louisa and left their box. Meg and Louisa took their seats once more.

"Are you well?" Meg asked in a whisper.

Louisa simply nodded.

"I cannot believe he followed you here," Meg continued. "Not to worry though. I shall help you be rid of him, just like at the masquerade."

It was the least she could do after all the help Louisa had been to her over the past few days. But when her friend made no response, merely focused more intently on the performance finally beginning below, Meg frowned. Was Louisa behaving so strangely because of Mr. Abbott's sudden appearance? Or was something else upsetting her? Miss Wells and Matthew perhaps?

Meg couldn't blame Louisa for her silence when she herself wasn't feeling up to speaking either, especially when the performance proved to be the longest of her life.

When it finally ended, Meg was so emotionally spent from trying to keep her mind and eyes from straying toward Matthew that she didn't say a word in the carriage, feigning sleep until they reached Hollridge. Once inside, Louisa silently departed to her room, and Meg went straight to bed, hoping rest would provide her with the respite she desperately needed.

But no relief came, for as she tried to sleep, her mind raced faster than Miss Michaels on ice skates. Eventually, she gave up, pulling on her dressing gown and tiptoeing through the corridors toward Louisa's room where light shone forth from the bottom of the door.

"Louisa? Are you awake?" she asked, tapping on the door.

A moment passed before she replied. "Yes. You may come in."

Meg slipped into the room, closing the door behind her with a soft click. The light from the fireplace and the single candle flickering on Louisa's bedside table cast low shadows around the room. Louisa sat up in her bed, leaning against a pillow and the headboard. She lowered her book and greeted Meg with a weak smile.

"Can you not sleep either?" Meg asked, motioning to the book as she crossed the room.

"I'm afraid not."

Meg sat at the foot of the bed, tracing circles in the flower pattern of Louisa's cover. "Are you worrying about Mr. Abbott?"

"Among other things."

Meg paused. "What other things?"

Louisa pulled her eyes away. Her voice was so soft, Meg had to lean closer to hear her. "My brother."

Of course, Louisa was upset with his behavior toward Meg that evening. She was such a dear friend, always concerned for the well-being of others.

"I suppose we shall simply have to work a little harder to draw his attention to me then," Meg said, attempting light-heartedness.

"Or...or perhaps we ought to stop inflicting our will on him and let him choose his life for himself."

Meg stared. "What do you mean?"

As Louisa met her eye, her solemn expression pressed the truth into Meg's mind. "You..." Meg swallowed. "You no longer wish for me to marry your brother?"

Louisa leaned forward, grasping Meg's hand in her own. Her cold fingers sent icy threads up Meg's arm. "Of course I do. I wish to call you my sister more than anything. I only feel as if perhaps we have become a little carried away with our matchmaking."

Meg's mind was spinning, creating a dizziness worse than when she and Matthew had spun together on the ice. If Louisa still wished for Meg to marry Matthew, why was she telling her to stop pursuing him? Was she truly more upset with Meg's attention to Matthew than with Mr. Abbott following her from London?

"What has brought about this change?" Meg breathed, her back beginning to curve like an evergreen bough heavy with snow.

Louisa's words were soft, barely louder than the snapping fire in the hearth. "It was something Miss Warren said last night, that Matthew and Miss Josephine were taken with each other."

Frustration simmered within Meg. She pulled her hand away from Louisa. "So you believe her words? You believe your brother has formed an attachment with Miss Josephine? I can assure you that he has not."

The truth of their kiss was at the tip of her tongue, ready to fall off in an instant, but Meg pulled it back. She had longed to tell Louisa, but after Matthew's less-than-ideal reaction to their affection, she'd been too fearful to admit their kiss aloud.

"No, I don't believe that in the slightest," Louisa said. "But I...I don't believe he has formed an attachment with *anyone* over Christmastide."

The words penetrated Meg's defenses, frozen daggers stabbing at her already battered heart. She stood from the bed, moving closer to the hearth. "I see. Anyone, including myself."

"I hope you know why I say such a thing, Meg. It is only to protect you. To keep you from becoming hurt, should you place too much hope in his falling in love with you. I could never forgive myself if I pressured either one of you into a relationship that would never work. It would hardly be fair."

Meg nodded, chewing on her bottom lip to keep her senses about her. "So you think I am being unfair in my treatment of him? That a relationship between us would never work? Do you think I am feigning my love? Treating this as a game?"

Louisa pushed back her covers and moved to stand beside Meg. "No, not at all. I know you have sincere feelings for him. But ever since Christmas, you've changed. You are no longer lighthearted and carefree. It is as if...as if you are obsessed over capturing his love."

Obsessed? *Capturing* his love? Meg huffed out a disbelieving breath. They'd had slight disagreements before, but Louisa would simply walk away and keep her frustrations to herself. Now, however, she was speaking so openly, Meg could hardly believe her ears.

"This is not a game for me, Louisa."

"In a way it is. At times, I feel as if you push so hard to have your own feelings known, you forget others have their own will."

"When have I done this?" Meg asked, her voice raising.

Louisa lifted her hands out to her side in a weakened stance. "You are doing so right now. You tell me you will help me be rid of Mr. Abbott when I don't know if I *want* to be rid of him."

Meg pulled back, her brow furrowed. "You have feelings for the squirrel?"

"I am twenty-one, Meg. I cannot stay unmarried forever."

"But to have to settle with—"

"I would not be settling, I…" Louisa broke off with a sigh, pressing a hand over her eyes.

Meg stared at her incredulously. How could Louisa wish to be with the man? She'd never mentioned a word about him, only that he was serious-minded. Mr. Abbott wasn't unattractive by any means, but was he not the dullest person they'd ever met? Louisa, wish to marry him? Meg could hardly believe it.

"Never mind that now," Louisa continued, drawing Meg's attention to the present. "I speak only out of the deepest love for our friendship when I say that either Matthew wishes to be with you, or he does not. You cannot force someone to fall in love with you, Meg."

Meg's mouth fell open in surprise. "I-I'm not forcing him. I'm merely helping him to see…" She ended with a sigh.

Louisa didn't understand. She must be simply confused after seeing Mr. Abbott that evening. She couldn't love that man, just like she couldn't truly believe that Meg would force Matthew to love her.

With a sinking feeling in her heart, Meg backed away toward the door. Matthew *would* love Meg. He just needed her help. Didn't he?

She shook her head. "I'm sorry to have burdened you with this, Louisa. You may rest assured I shall not any longer."

And without another word, she fled from the room. Louisa didn't call after her.

As Meg returned to her room, she plopped onto her bed with a frustrated groan. How could Louisa believe Meg was simply playing a game, essentially trying to trick Matthew into falling in love with her? Meg genuinely loved Matthew. Why would she ever trick him into doing something he didn't wish to do?

She brought her thumb to her mouth, chewing on her nail as her eyes wandered to her dresser, where rested on top the small, white berry Matthew had handed her from the kissing bough.

He'd enjoyed kissing her, she knew that. But was his avoidance of her that day not proof enough that he regretted the action? What if, by that kiss, he feared that Meg loved him, a feeling he could not reciprocate?

And what if, for reasons Meg couldn't understand, Louisa *did* have feelings for Mr. Abbott? Had Meg ever asked her? Or had she just assumed all the blushing and downcast eyes were due to Louisa's dislike of the man—rather than her love of him?

She winced, regret settling deep in her heart. She'd done terrible things. She'd pushed her will on her friend. And she'd tricked Matthew into kissing her because she'd wanted it for herself. Never mind that he'd tried to prevent it a number of times. She hadn't had a care what her friends felt or thought. She hadn't since the masquerade and she'd pulled Louisa away from Mr. Abbott and forced Matthew to dance with her, though she knew he disliked the pastime.

If Meg truly loved Louisa, she would let her choose her own future. And if Meg truly loved Matthew, she should be happy for him if he found a woman whom he wished to marry. If he *didn't* love Meg, then she needed to accept it.

Drawing in a deep breath, she rose from her bed and retrieved the berry from the dresser, clasping it in her palm and lumbering toward the window. With a heavy hand, she pushed the black-leaded pane open. The cold air burned her lungs, but it was a welcome relief to the bitter remorse stinging her heart.

Louisa was right. It *had* been an obsession for Meg. She'd feared not possessing Matthew's love, not remaining in his family, and having to stay with hers. But it wasn't fair anymore. She would no longer make Matthew or Louisa a pawn.

She stuck her hand out of the window, the berry trembling in her palm before she tipped it to the side, and her supposed pearl dropped to the ground.

She loved Matthew and Louisa. It was time to show it by asking after Louisa's true feelings. It was time to show it by letting Matthew go, by allowing him to be happy with whom he chose. Tomorrow, she would apologize to Louisa, she would begin her life anew.

And if Matthew didn't love her, she would find someone who did.

CHAPTER 8

"*A*h, here they are."

Matthew's heart tapped against his chest at Mother's words. He knew of whom she spoke. He and his parents had been waiting for Meg and Louisa to come down from their rooms for nearly ten minutes now. At this rate, they would most certainly be late for the musicale at the Lincolns'. Not that he cared. He was mostly just trying to find a distraction to keep himself from looking up at Meg. He was afraid one glance would ruin his resolve to forget about what had occurred between them.

Nothing had happened, of course, apart from what naturally occurred beneath a kissing bough. Their kiss was completely normal, and he'd enjoyed it as much as any man would. Never mind that he had lingered or that he hadn't been able to keep himself from thinking of it for longer than a few minutes at a time. He simply needed to ignore his overworking heart, especially right now, as her slippered feet came closer and closer toward him.

"We must apologize for our delay," Louisa said as they reached the bottom of the stairs. "We were speaking and lost track of time."

Matthew noted their shared smiles and linked arms out of the corner of his eye. Of what had they been speaking?

"I also had to change my gown again," Louisa continued. "The other one didn't match with Meg's quite as nicely. This one does, though, wouldn't you agree?"

"Oh, surely," Mother said. "You two look as beautiful as always."

Matthew watched from the corner of his eye as Father placed a soft kiss to each of the girls' hands. "You know, there are times when I do believe you and Meg are the twins, instead of you and Matthew. Wouldn't you agree, son?"

Matthew focused intently on smoothing out his jacket sleeve. "Indeed. Shall we depart? The Lincolns will be awaiting our arrival."

"Since when have you ever been anxious to depart for a social gathering?" Father asked, a smile in his voice.

"Since I discovered that it would help me reach home sooner," Matthew returned.

"But, Matthew, you didn't even look at us," Louisa said. "Come now, or we shall refuse to leave the Lincolns' home this evening and keep you there forever."

Matthew sighed. He supposed determining not to look at Meg ever again was rather ridiculous, seeing as how she practically lived with them. Very well, he would take one glance at their gowns then look away. Under no circumstances would he stare or allow his thoughts—or heart—to run rampant again.

With steely determination, he finally looked up. And immediately, he failed.

He barely looked at Louisa before taking in the sight of Meg's glowing white gown, red ribbon laced around her bodice, delicate pearls around her neck, and cheeks as rosy as her curved lips. One look was all it took, and the feelings he'd tried so hard to repress took residence once more in his confused, swirling heart.

This was why he'd been avoiding her, to prevent the heat rushing through his body and flushing his face. Why was he feeling this way at the mere sight of her? And why did she appear so completely the opposite? Her smile was easy, her stare stalwart. She didn't fidget as he did. Did that mean she hadn't felt any change since their kiss?

Disappointment rooted in his chest for reasons he couldn't begin to understand.

"So?" Louisa's voice echoed through his mind.

"They could be sisters, could they not?" sounded Mother's voice next.

Matthew still stared. Just like he'd told himself not to. He blinked, pulling his eyes away and clearing his throat. "Yes, just like sisters."

And yet, they were nothing like sisters, for that would make Meg *his* sister. And he'd certainly never had such musings for Louisa as he now had for Meg.

He shook his head. His feelings were superfluous, nothing short of a simple reminder that she was an attractive female, a reminder of the party spirit they'd both been affected by that late, New Year's Eve night. He would do good to forget it.

"Shall we?" he asked, making headway for the door.

The carriage ride took longer than he'd hoped, especially with Meg seated right across from him. Each time their knees bumped together or their eyes met, he ignored his traitorous, quickening heart and refocused his attention on the task before him.

Despite his sudden and strange notice of Meg, the bargain with his parents still stood. He couldn't believe he was almost completed with Mother's list. With number seven—Miss Wells—having been seen to the night before at the theatre, Matthew only had two women remaining. He didn't know much about number eight, a Miss Lincoln visiting her aunt and uncle over the winter, but Mother had warned him that she rather enjoyed speaking.

Matthew had brushed her cautioning aside, figuring any amount of speaking would be better than the silent Miss Wells, whom he'd only managed to pry a few sentences from the night before.

But, oh, how wrong he was. He was certain he'd never met a woman who spoke as quickly or as much as Miss Lincoln. Almost upon crossing the threshold of the Lincolns' drawing room, the young woman was upon him, speaking right after introductions before he'd even straightened from his bow.

"Oh, I'm so pleased you've come, Mr. Pratt," she said, her words blurring together in one, continuous stream, like water pouring from a glass. "My aunt has told me so much about you and your kind family. She also tells me you are not one for social gatherings. I must say, I am not so very fond of socializing with great crowds either, so you and I are similar in that regard. In fact, I've decided that I shall cling to you the majority of the night so we may take comfort in each other's presence, knowing we are both terribly out of place. Will that suffice?"

Matthew stared, dumbfounded. Mother hadn't been lying. Miss Lincoln *did* enjoy speaking. "I-I suppose that will do," he said.

"Excellent, then I shall enjoy the evening even more so with you at my side. Do you know, I'm quite looking forward to this now. My aunt says we shall have the best women singing this evening. Though, I am one of those who will be playing the pianoforte, and I must say, I do not consider myself a very great performer. My aunt does dote on me, as much as my own mother does. I do think it a duty, if not a requirement, to look after one's own female relatives. Why, your mother dotes on your sister, does she not?"

Matthew tried to keep up with her continual change of subject, slowly registering each of her words. He glanced to Louisa, hoping to share a look of humor, but she was no longer standing at his side. He looked around the room, spotting her and Meg standing with a few gentlemen. He returned his attention to Miss Lincoln, if only to distract himself from staring at Meg.

"Yes, I believe she does dote on my sister," he finally responded.

Her words took flight again, like a butterfly flitting about in the air, unsure of which direction to take as it continued in random patterns from side to side.

As she jumped from topic to topic, Matthew did his best to focus on what few words he could comprehend. Why did none of these women Mother had assigned to him know how to converse normally? Well, Meg did, of course. But then he'd always been comfortable speaking with her. Until that kiss had occurred.

His eyes found her across the room once again. She stood with her fingers laced together in front of her, accentuating her slim, feminine figure and long, slender arms.

He needed to keep his distance—and his eyes—from her that night. It would do him no good to stare.

Before long, though not soon enough for the sake of his ears, Miss Lincoln was pulled away by her aunt, and the musicale began. The guests made their way to the chairs lined up in four, straight rows facing the pianoforte.

Matthew moved to sit next to his family on the front row, but when he saw the only empty seat being at Meg's left, he paused. How could he sit next to her all evening, smelling that peppermint and risking the chance of their arms brushing up against each other? That wouldn't help him forget these ridiculous stirrings in his heart.

He would be better off sitting elsewhere, perhaps at the back of the room. He turned to retreat, but Miss Lincoln, who sat behind the Pratts with her aunt and uncle, reached her hand out toward him.

"Oh, Mr. Pratt, won't you sit here by us? I tell you, I'm excessively nervous, nearly more so then when I was ten years old and happened upon Lord Dalton last year in Town. My heart nearly leapt in fright. Oh, please tell me you will accept my offer. I could do with your calming presence. I'm sure I can hardly breathe with all of these strangers. Of course, you and I are not strangers, as we know just how the other is feeling. Please say you will sit beside me. I don't think—"

"Yes, very well." Matthew felt somewhat remorseful for interrupting, but honestly, he'd be standing through the whole musicale if he waited for the girl to stop speaking.

He lifted the program placed on the chair and took his seat beside her, facing forward. At once, his eyes fell directly on Meg's petite shoulders, elegant neck, and curled coiffure in front of him. He had the perfect view of her which would allow him to stare without the notice of others.

Sitting beside her would have been better than this.

Mrs. Lincoln stood from her seat and moved to the front of the room, speaking far slower than her niece. "Thank you all for joining us this wonderful evening. As you can see by the programs provided for you, we shall have a number of fine young ladies sharing their beautiful talents with us. All of the music played will be Christmas carols, to help us keep the spirit of the holidays alive. I do hope you will all have an enjoyable evening. First to bless us with her talent at the pianoforte will be Miss Paulson."

Miss Paulson moved to sit behind the instrument, followed directly by Mr. Richards, who would be helping her move the sheets of music. The dimple in his chin deepened as he smiled at Miss Paulson, who blushed in response.

Had they formed an attachment? That would certainly be a relief. Matthew had felt rather guilty for how attentive he'd been to her at Christmas. That was the one woman out of the nine who he'd feared giving the wrong impression to, that he liked her as more than a friend. Well, Miss Paulson, and now Meg, what with their kiss.

But then, Meg had been the one to request it.

As Miss Paulson's performance began, Matthew eyed the program to redirect his focus again. Seven performers. He wished there were more. Miss Lincoln couldn't speak when music was being played.

Amused with his own joke, Matthew almost wished he was seated beside Meg to share it. She would've appreciated it, though a necessary scolding swat would have accompanied her thinly veiled smile.

At the thought of Meg touching him, even with a pat, his cheeks warmed. He tried to straighten in his seat to view Miss Paulson, but his eyes continually fell to Meg's smooth jaw as she watched the performance herself.

He eyed the few, wispy curls that had slipped out of their pins and graced the skin at the nape of her neck. Would it make too much of a scene if he helped to pin them back up? He was only joking, of course. Mostly.

The music stopped. Miss Paulson stood and bowed her head to

the crowd now clapping. Matthew blinked. She'd finished already? He'd hardly heard a note played.

Miss Russell stood next, beginning her memorized performance of *While Shepherds Watched Their Flocks*. Matthew kept his eyes on his program. Now he longed for Miss Lincoln's conversation. With her quick tongue, he hardly had a moment to think about anything—or anyone—else.

He folded the edges of the program up and down, traced his fingers along the writing, and smoothed the paper between his palms until finally, the next three performances of the evening were completed.

When Meg and Louisa were announced to perform next, he grasped the program between his fingers so fiercely, the paper became as wrinkled as his cravat had been before Smith had insisted on pressing it that evening.

Keep your head down. There's no need to look up.

He looked up.

His eyes were drawn instantly to the fluttering of Meg's skirts as she made for the pianoforte. She sat down behind the instrument, and Louisa stood beside her.

As Meg arranged the sheets of music on the stand, Matthew waited with bated breath. She always looked to him right before a performance, seeking an encouraging nod. His stomach refused to settle at the thought of her blue eyes on him. Should he look away? No, that would be unthinkably cruel when she needed his help.

He placed a reassuring smile on his lips and waited for her eyes to find his. Except, they never did. Meg swept her gaze around the room with confidence, skipping right past Matthew, then began playing their piece, *The First Noel*.

Matthew's brow twitched. Why had she not looked at him? Months had passed since he'd been present to watch her perform anywhere, what with his being away at university, but still, did she not need his encouragement any longer?

He tried to brush aside his disappointment, but the dismissal bothered him more than he cared to admit.

Deciding instead to focus on the music, Matthew listened to his sister's smooth voice as she sang out the words to the Christmas carol. Meg said her own voice couldn't compare to Louisa's, which was why she always accompanied instead, but Matthew disagreed. He almost preferred Meg's slightly lower tone.

Without realization, his eyes returned to hers. How graceful she looked as she played, the candlelight flickering on her face, brightening her pink cheeks and dancing against her curls.

The music. Pay attention to the music.

But he couldn't. All he could think about was Meg and the warmth burgeoning within him like a sunrise.

When the music finally ended, Matthew clapped with the others, but only Louisa looked at him as the girls returned to their seats. Meg merely sat down without a glance in his direction. As she took her place in front of him, her wrap slid down the side of her chair, falling where his outstretched foot rested.

Before he had the chance to reach down and recover the wrap for her, her slender, gloved hand slid between her chair and the one beside her. As she felt around for the fabric, her fingertips nearly brushed against Matthew's shoe. He pulled his leg back, his heart flapping wildly before she found the wrap and slid it around her petite shoulders.

Only vaguely aware of Miss Lincoln moving to the pianoforte next, Matthew chewed the inside of his cheek, eying the back of Meg's head. As her friend, he needed to tell her what a fine job she'd done playing, did he not?

At the risk of the Lincolns becoming cross at him for speaking during their niece's performance, Matthew leaned forward and tapped Meg's left shoulder.

She tipped her head to the side, though her eyes didn't meet his.

"You played very well," he whispered. "As you always do."

Her lips raised, but she didn't respond, merely facing forward once more. He paused, leaning forward again. "Have you—"

"Excuse me."

Matthew pulled back as Mr. Kempthorne slipped into the seat beside Meg—in Matthew's seat.

"Do you mind if I sit here?" the vicar asked Meg in a whisper.

She shook her head with a bright smile then faced Miss Lincoln at the pianoforte.

Matthew leaned back in his chair, eying the vicar, as the vicar, in turn, eyed Meg. What was the man doing, moving places in the middle of a performance? That was far worse than Matthew's speaking. So inconsiderate of Miss Lincoln.

Miss Lincoln. When had she started playing? Matthew narrowed his eyes to look past Meg and focus on his number eight. The speed with which the girl spoke had nothing on how quickly her fingers now darted across the keys as she played the piece Matthew couldn't even recognize.

He tried very hard to listen, but his eyes dropped to Mr. Kempthorne, who leaned toward Meg, whispering something in her ear. Meg smiled, nodding her head in response as her curls bounced up and down.

Matthew tugged at his cravat. Why had he allowed it to be tied so tightly? And why was it so blasted hot in the room?

As Miss Lincoln's piece came to an end, he barely managed to give her an appreciative nod before Mr. Kempthorne spoke once again to Meg. The vicar was being very thoughtless to keep drawing her attention away from the other performers.

But then, why did Matthew care?

Without an answer, he became increasingly unsettled until the final performance of the night was complete, and each of the young ladies who had played or sung stood at the front of the room for a final ovation. Afterward, he tried to reach his sister and Meg before anyone else, but as the party surrounded the performers, and Miss Lincoln latched to Matthew's side like a lapping puppy, he lost the opportunity.

Instead, he drank his tea brought around by the footmen and listened to Miss Lincoln go on and on about how her fingers had trembled during her performance and now ached terribly. All the while Matthew's eyes wandered to Meg and Mr. Kempthorne, who now spoke alone together at the far side of the room.

Of what were they speaking? No doubt something dull and vicar-like. Where was Miss Russell when they needed her, with all her knowledge of the scriptures? She would enjoy Mr. Kempthorne far more than Meg was. Although, Meg's laughter did seem genuine. But there was no earthly way she could be entertained with a man the likes of Mr. Kempthorne. She was probably just trying to be nice.

Well, he would help her escape. Just as soon as he managed to escape himself.

"I do think I shall have to put a cold compress on my fingers after tonight's performance," Miss Lincoln was saying. "I fear I may have overdone it, but I do not regret playing. I'm fortunate my aunt convinced me to do so. Now I shall simply have to rest my hands, or I shall lose the use of them completely, what with how often I have practiced for this evening. You know, I—"

"My mother is quite a skilled pianoforte player," Matthew interjected, seeing his chance to escape and running with it before the subject changed again. "In fact, she was the one who taught Miss Baker and my sister to play. I'm certain she has a few suggestions for how to better rest your fingers. Why do you not ask her now?"

Miss Lincoln shook her head. "Oh, I wouldn't dream of bothering her, if she is as talented as you say she is. I am not so very confident to approach her. At any rate, I feel—"

"There's no need to be frightened," he said, taking her empty teacup from her hand and placing it on a nearby table with his own. "She will be more than happy to help you, I'm certain."

Miss Lincoln opened her mouth, no doubt to protest, but Matthew brazenly wrapped her hand around his arm and pulled her across the room toward his mother.

"Mother, Miss Lincoln wishes to speak with you," he said, ignoring Mother's arched eyebrows and Miss Lincoln's stunned-into-silence expression, leaving the women faster than he'd arrived.

As he walked away, he released a pent-up sigh. Mother could disapprove all she liked. He wouldn't need to speak another word to Miss Lincoln the rest of the night, for he'd learned enough about her to last a lifetime.

Gathering his energy that had been laid out on the floor with Miss Lincoln's chattering, Matthew glanced around the room until he found Louisa. He motioned her toward him with a subtle toss of his head.

"What is it?" she asked when she reached his side.

He nodded toward Meg. "Our friend is in need of a rescue."

Louisa followed his eyes to where Meg laughed with the vicar. "Why? She looks to be enjoying herself."

Matthew scoffed. Did Louisa know Meg at all? "She's clearly putting on a performance. She'd never be so entertained by Mr. Kempthorne, especially for so long."

The man had hardly left her side all evening. Matthew usually did the very same, of course, but that was different. Meg *wanted* Matthew by her side. She couldn't want the vicar with her.

"Are you well this evening, Matthew?" Louisa asked. "You appear a little flushed."

"Of course I am well. Apart from being upset for the sake of our friend. She's clearly uncomfortable speaking with him."

"Is she? Or are *you* uncomfortable with it?"

He pulled a face, maintaining his watchful eye in Meg's direction. "Whatever can you mean?"

He barely registered his sister's silence before she patted him on the shoulder. "I'm afraid you are on your own with this, Matthew. I wish you luck."

And with that, she turned and walked away.

Matthew churned over her words before disregarding them with annoyance. She wasn't being very helpful that evening, but what did it matter? If she wasn't willing to rescue Meg, Matthew was.

He drew a deep breath and strode toward the couple—toward Mr. Kempthorne and Meg, who were decidedly not a couple—with a determined step. As he approached, he met Mr. Kempthorne's eyes, and the vicar straightened, his hands clasped behind his back.

"Good evening, Mr. Pratt."

Meg turned around, her smile instantly dimming. She must be completely exhausted, filled with relief to see Matthew coming to her rescue.

"Good evening," Matthew returned, looking to Meg. "I do hope I am not interrupting."

"Not at all," Mr. Kempthorne said. Did the man answer for Meg now? "I was simply telling Miss Baker here of my time at school."

"Oh, I hope you are finished," Matthew joked. "I fear I've had enough schooling to last a lifetime." How true his statement was. He was only continuing his schooling to avoid Mother's constant badgering. Now that she promised to stop, he would be able to finish this final term and live out his life comfortably from home.

Mr. Kempthorne smiled. "Perhaps one day you may grow to learn and appreciate the chance you have to educate your God-given mind, Mr. Pratt. Heaven knows I finally have."

Matthew stiffened. He glanced to Meg, who took a sip of her tea with eyes averted. She was still looking for an escape. How had Matthew forgotten? "My sister is like me and is quite convinced that I do not need to educate myself further. Perhaps you may speak with her now about your own view on the matter, Mr. Kempthorne."

The vicar glanced to Meg, clearly hesitating to leave her. "Well, we are all free to form our own opinions, are we not?"

"Of course. My own belief will not change, but you may be able to convince Louisa to change hers." Matthew turned to the side, motioning across the room toward his sister. "She so often cries when I depart, and though I agree with her sentiments, I would appreciate any assistance you might offer in ensuring her happiness."

With a fleeting glance at Meg, the vicar finally nodded. He tipped his head in departure then crossed the room toward Louisa. Matthew watched him leave with a satisfied smile. That would teach his sister to help when next he asked for it.

"What do you think you are doing?" Meg asked beside him.

He turned toward her, ready to receive her gratitude, but at her sharp tone and lowered brow, he leaned back. "What do you mean?"

"Why did you send him away?" she asked in a vehement whisper.

She was angry? Whatever for? "I-I thought that was what you wished me to do."

She released an incredulous huff, and his cheeks warmed. "Did I give the impression that I was unhappy with his company? Or were my smiles and laughter not obvious enough of my pleasure?"

Matthew glanced around them, lowering his voice to avoid the attention from others. "I sincerely thought I was helping. How could I have known you would wish to speak with the vicar, of all men?"

She placed her teacup aside and propped her hands on her hips. Where was that smile that made her eyes shine, the one she'd shared with Mr. Kempthorne? "Why is it so very difficult to believe that I would wish to speak with him? He's a fascinating gentleman."

"Fascinating?" he said with as much shock as if Meg had just admitted to actually despising the cold, which would have been more believable. "You and Louisa have only ever spoken of how dull he is."

"Hush," she scolded. "That is not true. We speak far more of how kind and handsome he is, and humorous."

Matthew's jaw tightened, his fists clenched together. He glanced over his shoulder at Mr. Kempthorne, who was now speaking with a very red-faced Louisa—even redder than when that Mr. Abbott found her in the theatre.

Mr. Kempthorne was slightly more broad-shouldered than Matthew, but the vicar wasn't *that* much taller than him. How could Meg find him attractive? How could she find him *humorous*?

Matthew turned to face her again, anger sparking inside him. Why was he reacting in such a way? Normally, he could brush aside his frustrations. Now, he felt out of breath, though all he was doing was preventing himself from marching straight up to the vicar to demand he say something wittier than Matthew. He highly doubted the man could.

"Well, forgive me," he said to Meg, "I was unaware that you had feelings for the man."

She stared up at him in silence. Not a word of contradiction. Did that mean…

He swallowed. "So you do feel something for him?"

"What is it to you if I do?"

He raised a cavalier shoulder, though his stomach contorted. "Nothing. I simply never thought you could be interested in a man of the church. But I suppose you have changed."

Her nostrils flared. "As have you. As I recall, the Matthew I grew up with would not choose to court half the women in Yorkshire."

Guilt shifted his conscience to the forefront of his mind, and his eyes dropped to the floor. Of course Meg would think such a thing. No doubt he was now a philanderer in her eyes. "I am not courting any woman in Yorkshire."

"Well you have fooled us all then. What with how you've been carrying on, I'd have thought you eager to jump forth into matrimony."

"I have no desire for my life to change in such a way." His tone fell flat. He wasn't sure *what* he wished for anymore.

"Well I wish for *my* life to change," she whispered, pointing at herself. "So I shall return to Mr. Kempthorne's side and speak with him for the rest of the night if I wish."

She raised her eyebrows, as if daring him to stop her. He clamped his mouth shut, refusing to fall for the bait, but when she took a step away from him, he reached out, grasping her arm.

"You can't," he said, unaware of what he was even saying. "He…he wouldn't make you happy."

But I would.

He squeezed his eyes shut to dispel the thought. He shouldn't be thinking such a thing. Not about his friend. Not when he wanted his life to remain the same.

His glove slipped against hers, and she pulled out of his grasp in a swift movement. "You do not have the right to say such a thing to me, Matthew Pratt. You are not my brother, nor are you my intended." She took a step closer, the smell of peppermint overpowering his senses. "And I will not wait forever."

Her blue eyes flashed, and his breathing stopped. Her words echoed in his mind, his heart thrumming against his ribs. Confusion clouded his judgment once more as his eyes dropped to her pink lips. He moved a fraction closer, but she shook her head and walked away, disappearing into the small crowd.

Matthew stared at the floor, ignoring the curious glances he received from the others near enough to have seen their heated argument.

What had she meant, she would not wait forever? For what, to change her life? To marry Mr. Kempthorne? He was repulsed by the very idea.

"You, my dear brother, are a fool."

Matthew started. Louisa? When had she moved to stand beside him? "What do you mean? Did you hear…"

"Yes, every word. And you're even more senseless than I thought."

He scowled, finding Meg across the room speaking once again with Mr. Kempthorne. "You are calling *me* senseless when Meg is the one who has gone and fallen in love with the vicar?"

Louisa scoffed. "She doesn't love the vicar. She loves…"

Matthew's attention whipped to his sister's. "Who?"

She simply shook her head. "I will not push you one way or another, brother, but after being witness to your behavior this evening, things are finally clear to *me*. As I said before, *you* are a fool." With a look of disappointment, she walked away.

"Louisa?"

She ignored him. He stifled a growl of frustration. What had she meant about pushing him, about his behavior? He contemplated hounding her until she responded to his questions. He wanted to know, *needed* to know who had won his friend's affection.

But when he glanced over his shoulder once more at Meg, his breathing hitched. Her eyes were upon him, wide. Revealing. Fire flamed within him, spreading throughout his limbs.

She quickly pulled her gaze away, but Matthew remained staring.

No, there was no earthly way it was possible. He imagined it. Louisa imagined it. But as the moments ticked by, the mists of confusion faded, and his thoughts cleared.

Meg loved…him?

Memories of the last few days flashed through his mind. How she'd blushed at his compliments, asked him to kiss her, behaved strangely each time he'd shown attention to another woman.

He placed a hand over his mouth, rubbing his forefinger over his upper lip. They had always been simply friends. Had it changed for her while he was at school? Was she pursuing the vicar because she thought he was interested in other women?

Was he interested in other women…or only with Meg?

Blast these cursed bargains. He never should have agreed to them.

He squeezed his eyes tightly closed. He needed to gain control of his thoughts. He only had one woman left after tonight. A simple kiss with Meg and a false thought that perhaps she was in love with him—and he with her—could not prevent him from success.

Yet, as her laughter drifted toward him, laughter induced from Mr. Kempthorne, Matthew's neck tightened, as if one movement might cause his spine to snap in two like a piece of gingerbread.

Very well. He did not know for certain if Meg had feelings for him or if he had feelings for her. But one thing was for certain, the mere thought of his best friend falling in love with another man was driving him quite certainly into madness.

CHAPTER 9

*M*atthew slowed his step as he approached the drawing room the next morning. He couldn't do this. He didn't have the courage to face her, not after all that had been revealed—or rather, hinted at—the evening before.

After the party, he'd spent half the night awake, stewing over his jealousy of Mr. Kempthorne and over Louisa's suggested information.

Matthew didn't know what to do. He'd never been jealous of other men before, especially concerning their attention to Meg. Then again, his heart had never pumped so forcefully when she'd entered a room, and his brow had certainly never sweat at the mere thought of her.

He pulled out his handkerchief, dabbing at his forehead. What was he to do with himself and with this information? And more importantly, how was their friendship to remain the same, how was his *life* to remain the same, with such a revelation?

He shook his head, tucking the cloth away and squaring his shoulders. He didn't have to make any life-altering decisions right now. After all, he wasn't about to pursue his newfound feelings if he wasn't certain Meg felt the same for him first. He trusted his sister, but what if she was wrong? He couldn't risk the possible rejection. If Meg did truly love him, well, then…he would decide what to do when the time came.

All he needed to do now was find the courage he'd misplaced that morning and be brave enough to speak with Meg. Or just look at her. Either would do for now.

With a resolute nod, Matthew strode down the corridor, but he paused again just outside of the room. This time, it was not from fear but anger. Anger produced from voices coming from the drawing room. Voices that should not be at Hollridge at all, but in Scotland.

Meg's parents. What the devil were they doing there? They weren't supposed to return to Haxby for months.

Mrs. Baker's smooth voice sailed toward Matthew as he remained out of sight. "How pleased I am to hear that you perform for others, Margaret. Though, I should like it if you would play for us at Stoneworth every now and again."

Matthew nearly bared his teeth at her use of Meg's given name, the name his friend had always hated. Matthew had been the one to suggest the use of a nickname, so 'Meg' had been born and used ever since by those who truly knew her.

Unlike her own parents.

Meg's voice was soft as she responded. "I've tried to play for you, Mother, but you always say Stoneworth causes the pianoforte to echo too loudly within its walls to sound pleasant."

Matthew could only imagine her downcast eyes. He couldn't bear the timidity in her tone. He needed to help her, to rescue her.

He froze at the word, pulling back. Rescue. He'd thought Meg had required help to escape Mr. Kempthorne the night before, and he'd been woefully mistaken. Perhaps he was wrong now, as well? Perhaps she truly had changed so drastically that she wished to be with her parents now?

But he couldn't remain outside, doing nothing forever. He would simply enter the drawing room and wait to offer his help until he knew for certain Meg wished for it.

With a slow and steady pace, he entered the room. Meg didn't meet his eyes. Was that due to her parents' arrival, or because of their argument last night?

"Mr. Matthew Pratt," Mrs. Baker said after Matthew bowed. "I am surprised to see you here, what with how often you are away at university."

His lips in a smile felt as unnatural as Meg being silent in their drawing room. "Well, I am surprised to see *you* both here. Did Scotland not suit this year?"

Mrs. Baker laughed. "Oh, heavens, no. It always suits. As do our dear friends the Malcolms. I trust you remember our mentioning them?"

How could Matthew—or anyone in Haxby, for that matter—forget? It was no secret the Bakers enjoyed the company of the glorious Malcolms to anyone in town, even their own daughter.

Mr. Baker held his hands behind his back. "We are simply here because, well, we have missed our dear Margaret so very much, we couldn't bear to be away from her any longer."

Matthew's eyes fell on Meg. Her smile was weak, even more so than Matthew's.

"Indeed," Mrs. Baker said. "We would have sent a letter, but that would have taken far too long to await her reply, so we have simply come in person to ask the question ourselves."

Matthew looked back to the Bakers. "Forgive me, what question?"

They looked expectantly at their daughter. Meg finally raised her eyes to meet his. They were cold, void of any emotion. "My parents have come to request my presence in Scotland for the remainder of the winter."

Matthew's lips parted, the breath pressing from his lungs. They were taking her away?

"Isn't it wonderful?" Mrs. Baker said, holding her hands to her chest. "We have always longed for Margaret to join us. How pleased we are that the time has finally arrived. You see, the Malcolms have a distant cousin that have come to stay with them this winter. He is very close to Margaret's age, and we believe she will make a wonderful addition to our now extended party. Isn't it wonderful?"

A near-tangible barrier separated the room. On one side, the Bakers smiled away, speaking about the pipers who would perform for them during their visit and about the sights in Edinburgh they would see. They were completely unaware of anyone but themselves. On the other side, Mother, Father, and Louisa remained silent, lips downcast and shoulders sunken as they listened to the Bakers piping on.

Between them all, Matthew stared at Meg. His heart was sinking fast, plummeting through the air with no end in sight.

Since she was a child, Meg had longed for her parents to bring her to Scotland, but they'd constantly denied her request. The Pratts were always left to comfort the crying Meg, who couldn't understand why her parents appeared to love the Malcolms more than her.

As she'd grown older, her tears had shifted, appearing instead when her parents would return, for then she would have to live with them at Stoneworth, forever in the shadows of the memory of the Malcolms.

Now, with the invitation to join her parents in Scotland finally extended, Meg should have been pleased, and Matthew for her. So why was she on the verge of tears, her chin trembling and fingers clasped together on her lap? And why was Matthew fighting his desire to pull her in his arms and beg her to stay?

Was it because neither of them wanted her to join her parents? Because they did not wish her to leave the Pratts? Or because they did not wish to leave each other?

"And, oh, the Malcolms are sure to enjoy your company now," Mrs. Baker said. "They have always longed to—"

"When?" Matthew blurted out. Mrs. Baker turned to him with a disapproving brow. He cleared his throat. "Pardon me, but when are you to return to Scotland?"

"At our earliest convenience," Mr. Baker responded. "We know Margaret enjoys the holidays here at Hollridge, and I understand your family is hosting the Twelfth Night revels this year, so we shall leave the morning after."

Two days? He had two days left with Meg? Matthew had an

entire week before he would return to school, an entire week he'd thought he'd be able to spend with Meg, now that his bargain with Mother was nearly complete.

He ground his teeth together. That blasted, cursed bargain. If he hadn't wasted every moment with the chattering, preaching, dull women, he could have spent more time with Meg. Now she was leaving, and he didn't want her to.

But did she?

Her eyes were still lowered, but when she reached up to swipe a quick hand at her cheek, he knew she was brushing away tears. Tears born from her parents' arrival, tears born from their sudden attention. Attention that should have been there from the start.

He stared down at her, willing her to look up at him until slowly, her eyes met his. The pain within them pierced his heart. He longed to embrace her, to tell her everything was well, to do something, anything, to have her smile return, as he did when they were children.

But with their families in the room, all he could do was remain where he stood. "I'm sorry," he mouthed out to her, praying for her to find the comfort she so desperately needed.

She looked away, the tendons in her neck standing out as she drew in a deep breath. Then suddenly, she stood, excusing herself with a bobbed curtsy and tearing from the room.

The Bakers stared at the empty doorway, stunned. The Pratts exchanged concerned glances. Matthew nearly darted from the room after her, but Mrs. Baker's words stopped him.

"Why, whatever is the matter with that girl?"

Matthew's parents eyed each other in search of an explanation, but Matthew's anger surged. "Can you not see? She doesn't wish to go—"

"Oh," Louisa interrupted with wide eyes. "I believe Meg spoke of writing a letter this morning to a friend in London. She must have forgotten to send it earlier. I'm sure she did not wish to interrupt you."

"Well, she did," Mrs. Baker muttered, glancing to her husband. "I had hoped her impetuous behavior would have been worked out by now, what with living here for so long. The Malcolms certainly won't approve of such conduct. Neither will their cousin." She turned to Matthew's mother. "I do hope her bad behavior has not troubled you over the years."

Matthew fisted his hands, his nails digging into his palms. How he wished to pull the woman from her seat and shake sense into her. Did she not realize the true reasoning behind Meg's departure? Did she not realize how she was hurting their only daughter? How they were always hurting her?

"I assure you, Meg has been nothing but a pure delight in our home," Mother responded. "We are certainly sorry to see her leaving so soon."

Mother must have seen Matthew's reddened face and growing scowl, for she glanced at him then sent a quick toss of her head toward the door.

Matthew understood in an instant. Without hesitation, he left the drawing room behind and went in search of Meg. He strode down the corridor, calling out her name until he reached the front hall and saw her dress disappear around the corner at the top of the stairs.

"Meg? Wait a moment, please."

When she didn't respond, he darted up the steps two at a time, pausing once he reached the top of the stairs. Meg hadn't gone into her room, as he'd expected. Instead, she stood gazing out of the large window in the corridor, overlooking the frozen gardens of Hollridge.

Slowly, he moved to join her, but her eyes remained fixed outside. The clouded skies and snow-covered countryside cast a white light across Meg. Her blonde curls shone brightly, and her nose and cheeks were as red as the berries they'd gathered for the house. Only this redness was caused from her tears, not the cold.

"Are you well?" he asked.

She nodded, though she didn't say a word.

"I'm so sorry they've come. Had you any warning?"

"No. They arrived this morning, while I was alone in the drawing room." She dropped her eyes to the window ledge she leaned up against. "They are quite adamant that I join them. They spoke to me at length about the Malcolms' cousin before your family joined us. My parents think that he and I...that we would make a fine match."

Matthew flinched at the deep ache inside him, as if someone were carving a hole in his chest to tear out his heart.

This was the true meaning behind her parents' return. They had finally found a reason to care for their daughter—because she would provide them a way to become family with the Malcolms. He didn't need to wonder if Meg was aware of their intentions. Her watery eyes and sunken shoulders spoke of how she felt on the issue.

Still, he couldn't assume she was as disgusted by this revelation as he was. The only way to know for certainty was to ask. "And... what do you think about their plans?"

She glanced at him sidelong. "You know me well enough, Matthew, to know how I feel. I wish to join my parents and the Malcolms no more than I wish to be coerced into a marriage purely for the sake of my parents' desire for familial ties."

Matthew knew the truth before she spoke it, but hearing it aloud patched the missing pieces in his chest, allowing his heart to resume its steady beating. "So you won't be joining them then?"

She lifted her arms half-heartedly in a shrug. "I don't know. I suppose I must, though, for what other choice do I have?"

You can remain here.

Matthew shook the thought from his mind, turning away to stare at the trees in the distance. Heavy snow fell from the upper branches, sending the rest of the snow to cascade in a white waterfall to the ground.

He knew Meg had secretly been longing for an invitation from her parents for years. If not to join them, at least to purely be thought of. For him to now suggest she remain at Hollridge simply because he wished her to, when he would be leaving shortly for school, would be unthinkably selfish.

"You know you have other choices, Meg, and I believe you know what they are. But I can speak for my parents and Louisa in saying that we want you to do what *you* wish to do. Though, I cannot say the same for your parents."

She hung her head. "I am well aware of the goodness of your family, and the lack thereof in my own. But I must learn to accept that I am a mere burden to my parents, unless I marry into the Malcolm family."

Matthew's heart dropped in unison with the single tear falling from Meg's eyelashes to the window ledge below. He reached out with a soft finger, raising her chin until her eyes met his. He hadn't touched her so softly since their kiss, and memories of their affection swirled in his mind.

"You needn't do such a thing if it causes you unhappiness." He ran his thumb along her smooth chin. "And they may wrongfully assume you are a burden, but you must know that my family has never thought of you in such a way."

She licked her lips, the moisture left behind causing his breathing to shallow. "And you? Do you think of me as a burden?"

He searched her eyes, still glassy from her tears. "I could never. You are family, dear Meg."

He trailed his thumb along her jawline, ending at the base of her ear.

"Like family," she breathed. "Like…like Louisa?"

The words echoed through his ears and down into his heart. He knew what she asked—did he still think of her as a sister?

Did he? Or was she more, far more than that now? His heart whispered the truth, but his fear, his desire to keep things the same, fought against it.

His lips parted, but no sound came forth. He was frozen, staring dumbly at the woman whose heart had already been broken by her parents, whose heart was now being trampled on by the man who was supposed to be her friend.

She blinked, realization donning in her blue eyes. She withdrew from his touch with a whisper. "I see. I understand now."

She couldn't understand, not when Matthew didn't even understand himself. "No, Meg. I…"

"That is perfectly fine," she said, a trembling smile on her lips.

"I-I understand, I do. And all is well. Excuse me, but I must return to my parents."

She turned, and panic twisted around Matthew's heart like a rope, one end pulling him toward Meg, the other pulling him back toward that fear of change he could not easily untie.

"Meg, please."

He could say nothing more, his mind and heart in turmoil as she disappeared around the corner. Her footsteps pattered down the stairs, drawing farther away from where he still stood, paralyzed by the fear that he would make the biggest mistake of his life either by following her—or by letting her go.

CHAPTER 10

*M*eg looked out of her bedroom window, staring at the stars, bright pinholes in a blackened sky. The moon's soft glow cast its light across the snowy landscape below, brightening the world's darkness. She'd always enjoyed Twelfth Night revels, but that evening, she wished to remain there, alone in her room with her thoughts.

Loneliness was far preferable to what awaited her downstairs—parents who did not love her, and a gentleman who was too afraid to. She did not relish the prospect of spending winter with her parents and the Malcolms, nor of meeting the gentleman they clearly wished for her to marry, but it was more appealing than waiting at Hollridge for Matthew to return from school and *still* not love her.

She'd been so encouraged the night of the musicale, what with his jealousy over her time spent with Mr. Kempthorne, but after her last conversation with him, she knew he either loved her and was too afraid to admit it, or he did not love her and was too afraid to hurt her.

Meg pressed her head against the cold glass of the window, closing her eyes as she drew in a slow, deep breath. She loved

Matthew. So deeply it hurt. But she loved him enough to wish him a happy life with or without her. And she could move on. Someday.

A knock sounded at her door, and she turned in time to see Louisa poking her head inside her room, a smile lighting her face.

"Oh, Meg. You look beautiful."

Meg smoothed down her red skirts. "Thank you. As do you."

Louisa wore a soft yellow gown that reminded Meg of the sunshine, only Louisa's happy expression turned to one of sadness as she watched Meg. "Have you decided yet?"

Meg nodded. "Yes, I am to go with my parents."

Louisa stepped into the room, closing the door behind her. "I don't understand. Why do you not stay here with me at Hollridge?"

Meg lowered her eyes. "I appreciate the offer. Truly, I do. But I cannot remain here forever."

As wonderful as the idea sounded, Meg was speaking the truth. One day, Louisa would marry, as would Matthew, and Meg would be trapped forevermore at Stoneworth, witness to Matthew's happiness with his new wife day in and day out for the rest of her spinster life.

No. It would be far better for her to leave Haxby now. The Malcolms' cousin sounded like a good man. She was sure she could be happy with him—or with another gentleman she was sure to meet in Scotland—one day.

Louisa sniffed. "I understand, of course. But I cannot bear the thought of saying goodbye to you this evening, even if it is only until you return to us in the spring."

Meg didn't have the heart nor the courage to tell Louisa she had no intention of returning to Hollridge, at least without a husband. Instead, she raised her chin with a forced smile.

"Then let us not dwell on our parting just yet. We still have an entire evening together. Shall we not make it a memorable one?"

Louisa nodded resolutely. "Yes, yes, you are right. We shall enjoy ourselves to the fullest."

Meg led the way from her room. "Dance all of the dances. Flirt with all of the gentlemen."

"Eat all the food," Louisa added.

Meg sighed airily. "That is what I look forward to the most."

"As do I."

Meg watched her from the corner of her eye. "Are you certain you are not looking forward to seeing Mr. Abbott this evening more?"

Louisa swung her attention to Meg, her cheeks flushed before she stared straight ahead. "The food. Let us speak more of the food."

Meg smiled knowingly. After apologizing for their argument the night of the theatre, Meg had finally listened in shock to Louisa as she shared about her growing feelings for Mr. Abbott, borne from her heart, rather than from her growing older. Since then, Louisa had refused to say anything more about it, though Meg suspected that evening that her friend was about to lose her heart entirely to the gentleman.

Just as Meg had lost hers to Matthew.

She pushed the thought aside and continued down the corridor, arm-in-arm with Louisa.

Tonight, Meg would force herself to remain positive. She would pretend to be well, she would pretend to be more than happy following her parents to Scotland. And she would pretend that her heart was not breaking at the mere thought of leaving Matthew and her true family behind.

Matthew glanced to the stairs for what he was sure was the twelfth time, drumming his fingers against his leg. Where was she? Meg and Louisa were usually late, but not *this* late. Nearly all of the guests had arrived, and Mother was about to begin the first game of the evening.

He didn't know why he was so anxious to see Meg, what with their last meeting ending so terribly. He'd been so fearful of meeting her again that he'd avoided her for two days. But tonight was her last night at Hollridge, and he would never forgive himself if he wasted away another moment that could be spent with his friend.

His friend. They could still remain friends after everything, couldn't they? After all, that was what he wanted, to be friends. Anything more and his life would change in ways he wasn't sure he was comfortable with, and he wasn't ready for such a thing.

"Mr. Pratt?"

Matthew looked away from the stairs to Miss Mosely, who stood beside him, staring expectantly up at him. "Pardon?"

"I was asking if you were looking forward to the evening," she repeated in her smooth voice.

"Oh, yes. Very much so. I trust you are, as well?"

She nodded, her shining black curls bouncing with the movement. Mother had chosen a strong contender for the ninth and final woman on Matthew's list. Miss Mosely was the most sought-after female in Haxby. Not only was she wealthy and of good breeding, she was also kind and generous. Yes, any gentleman would count himself lucky to be asked to spend an entire evening with such a woman.

Yet, Matthew's eyes drifted again to the stairs. This time, he wasn't met with disappointment. Miss Mosely was a beautiful, kind woman, but she was no Meg.

He couldn't look away from her. Meg slowly descended the stairs to the front hall, her red dress cascading softly down her feminine form while white lace in intricate patterns stretched across the bodice. Her golden hair formed a halo around her head, and her movements were ethereal, angelic. Breathtaking.

Two days ago, his mind had been a storm of confusion and worry. He could not answer her question. But now, as her blue eyes met his, he knew the answer.

No. He did not consider Meg a sister. He considered her something far, far dearer. He considered her as someone he could—

"Mr. Pratt? Your mother is calling us into the ballroom. Shall we go?"

Matthew reeled. Thank goodness Miss Mosely had interrupted him. Who knew what he'd been about to think?

He escorted the woman into the ballroom, grateful to put distance between himself and Meg. He needed to remember the bargains he'd struck, the fact that after tonight, he'd be a free man —free on his horse, and free to keep his life unchanged for as long as he wished.

A large number of the party moved to the adjacent room to play card games, but more than twenty unmarried ladies and gentlemen convened in the ballroom, where Matthew's mother explained the rules of the game of characters. Matthew tried to slip away from the group a number of times, but with Miss Mosely paying close attention to him, as well as Miss Josephine's and Miss Michaels's eyes in his direction, he had little chance of success.

"Let us begin," his mother said, "each of you will draw a slip of paper from this bonnet or this top hat." She raised the headwear in her hands. "The character you will play will be written on your paper, and you are required to stay in character for the rest of Twelfth Night. Should one fail to do so, or should one call another by his given name and not his character's name, then he or she shall have to pay a forfeit." She paused, her eyes twinkling. "And I must warn you, the forfeits this evening may or may not involve a harmless kiss or two."

A few giggles scattered around the group, but Matthew closed his eyes with frustration. Mother must be upset with him for not falling in love with any of the nine and was now making a final effort to push him into matrimony. He was well aware that she thought marriage would be the solution to his finally accepting change in his life.

Well, if a kiss with Meg hadn't made him love *her*—because it hadn't, really—and make him want to change his way of life, then a simple kiss with other women wouldn't work either.

He ignored his tossing stomach at the thought of kissing a woman other than Meg and drew his character from the top hat. Unfolding it, he read the name with dread. Sir Harry Hoax. He had to be the worst character of the evening, duping women by pretending he loved them, only to drop them for another.

Was fate playing a cruel joke, telling him that he had done the very same to nine women? He'd done his best not to give them false hope, but…what had he done to Meg? And in turn, what had he done to himself?

He pushed aside the disconcerting thoughts and joined the large circle of guests forming to introduce their characters. He kept his eyes off Meg, though he could see her watching him from the corner of his eye.

"Think you can slip away for a moment?"

Matthew started at his father's whisper in his ear. He turned to see him moving toward the doorway. Matthew faced forward, glancing around the group. He would miss the introductions of the others' characters if he left now, but that hardly mattered. He wasn't planning on participating in the game for very long anyway. He never did. But could he escape without notice in the circle? Perhaps not by everyone, but by Mother, yes.

He waited until she turned her back before making his escape, soundlessly striding across the dance floor and slipping through the door without a glance behind him.

"What did you need, Father?" Matthew asked as he joined him in the front hall.

Father merely sent him a cryptic smile before motioning his head to the side. "Follow me."

They made their way to the front door, passing a few late-comers and sneaking out of the house. As they followed the emptied carriages around the corner of the house toward the stables, Matthew knew at once what Father had planned.

They stood outside the stables, and Father's smile grew. "Your prize, son."

Just then, a groom exited through the large doors, leading behind him one of the most spectacular horses Matthew had ever seen. The stallion's black coat glinted in the lamplight from a passing carriage, contouring his large muscles and the angles of his sleek face. His thick mane and tail blew haphazardly in a soft breeze, and as he clopped against the gravel, the feathers above his hooves fluttered up and down.

Matthew accepted the lead from the groom, shaking his head in awe. "He is magnificent, Father." The horse tossed his head with a whinny, and Matthew grinned. "And a spirited one at that."

"A perfect match for you," Father said with a chuckle.

The stallion stomped his hoof in the gravel again, and Matthew reached forward, soothing him with a low hum and soft rub to his forelock. "We shall become great friends, you and I," he whispered.

The horse snorted, air puffing around him, as his ears rotated from front to back. What a creature he was. Matthew had never seen his equal. Accomplishing his parents' tasks was well worth it, knowing this steed was now his.

He looked over his shoulder. "Thank you, Father. But I must ask, why do you give him to me now? I have hardly spoken with Miss Mosely this evening."

Father came up next to him, patting the horse's side. "I thought you deserved a little encouragement to finish off the night. Besides, I hardly think you will fall in love in a single evening, especially if you haven't in a fortnight." He paused, watching Matthew from the corner of his eye. "You *haven't* fallen in love with any of them, have you?"

Matthew scoffed, his throat growing suddenly dry. "Of course not. I told you your deal was easier than Mother's."

Father chuckled. Matthew stroked the horse's neck and avoided his gaze.

"Right," Father said. "I think we ought to return indoors now before your mother grows suspicious, yes? I hardly think she will appreciate me stealing you away at the beginning of her game."

"But I certainly appreciate it. I will join you in just a moment."

As Father made for the house, Matthew gripped onto the leather lead of the horse, struggling to maintain a similar hold of the excitement he felt slipping from his fingers.

What was the matter with him? He deserved this horse. He had worked hard for this horse. He had met with each of the women and hadn't fallen in love with a single one of them. So why couldn't he shake this ridiculous guilt, this feeling that he had just lied to himself and to his father?

He should be celebrating this evening. He had almost completed his parents' wagers. He was almost free. And yet, he felt more confined than ever. His fear of change had caged his spirit, prevented him from admitting what he truly wished for, *who* he truly wished for, in his life. And as magnificent as this stallion was, he wished for something, *someone*, more.

As the groom led the horse back into the stables, Matthew's heaviness increased, a darkness entering him blacker than the steed. He slowly made his way back to the house and into the ballroom, so dejected, he didn't notice his mother approaching him until she spoke.

"How nice of you to join us, Matthew," she said with an accusatory look. "Your character has been introduced for you. And, as we still have our bargain, I expect you to be attentive this evening to Miss Mosely and any other woman with whom you may come in contact. Understood?"

Matthew nodded, barely hearing her words.

"Matthew? Are you well?"

His eyes wandered about the room, a frown puckering his brow.

A moment passed by before Mother spoke again, her voice softer than before. "The characters of the king and queen this evening have requested for the dancing to begin early. Please, find a partner so there shall be no woman seated at the side tonight."

She gave his arm an encouraging squeeze then walked away, but Matthew hardly noticed. He was already watching the dancers in the middle of the ballroom, one dancer in particular.

Meg's cheeks were rosy as she weaved in and out of the couples in the set, the folds of her red gown and white ribbon fluttering as she danced to and fro. Once again, Matthew's breath was taken away at the sight of her.

He was not supposed to be staring at her. He was supposed to be finding a partner. But how could he be light on his feet when his heart was so unbearably heavy? How could he dance with anyone this evening, when the only woman he wanted to dance with was already occupied?

Slowly, the words sunk in, and his lips parted in surprise. The only woman he wanted to dance with was Meg.

He tore his eyes away from her, glancing out over the other dancers and realizing only then that the nine women from Mother's list were in attendance that evening, each of them now dancing before him.

Miss Paulson moved gracefully alongside her partner, Mr. Richards, her face aglow as she smiled up at him. Miss Michaels, just as she'd done on her skates, danced in quick movements, as if competing to see who could finish first.

Miss Russell was partnered with Mr. Kempthorne—a fine match for the vicar, as they were no doubt reciting scripture to each other—while Miss Warren danced beside her sister, looking rather bored. Miss Josephine, however, seemed to be enjoying herself as her hands lingered in her partner's far longer than necessary.

Miss Wells, as timid as she had been at the theatre, looked nearly ready to faint with her mouth clamped shut, the exact opposite of Miss Lincoln, whose mouth had yet to close as she spoke with her very wide-eyed partner in a constant stream of words. Miss Mosely, however, looked perfectly poised as she attracted the stares of a number of gentlemen, even those who had partners.

And then there was Meg. Meg, with whom he should have started, number one on his list, number one in his life. He did not realize until that moment how he'd compared her these last two weeks with each of the women listed, how he'd wanted to be with her instead of any of them.

Now, seeing these nine ladies dancing before him, he knew without a doubt he wished to dance with Meg more than any of them. He wished to dance with her, to *be* with her, because he was in love with her.

As a young man, Matthew had loved his way of life, enjoying the simplicity of a fixed, daily routine with Meg and his family. Going to university had upended his ease, bringing a storm of change to his life, but he always soothed his worries by reminding himself that those whom he loved would always be at home waiting for him.

But now, Meg was going to Scotland to marry another, and Matthew would end up without her.

As she waited her turn to dance down the set, her gloved hands clapped in time with his racing heart.

How selfish he was to think Meg would remain at Hollridge forever, without a husband and children, without a home that was truly hers—simply waiting on Matthew as he lived in his silly world where he believed he could prevent change from happening.

He had been a first-rate fool. He couldn't prevent change any more than he could prevent the sun from setting on a joyous day. But he *could* beg for Meg to remain, and he *could* change. For her.

For as fearful as he was of altering his life, the thought of losing his dear Meg was far more terrifying.

The moment the dance ended, Meg backed away from the group and slunk into a darkened corridor. As the cool air drifted toward her and her eyes adjusted to the darkness, she leaned against the wall and breathed a sigh of relief.

She almost wished Mrs. Pratt would have held a simple ball that evening, instead of all these games she had planned. Not wishing to offend her by refusing to play, Meg had agreed to join in with the festivities that evening, receiving the character of Kitty Coy, a woman fearful of gentlemen. It was perfect for her, really. This way, she could sneak away and hide alone for hours. And if she didn't wish to speak to a single gentleman that night, she had the excuse not to.

Of course, there was one gentleman she did wish to speak with, but she had not seen him since he'd snuck away from the circle of characters.

She squeezed her eyes shut, reminding herself of her determination not to dwell on Matthew that night. If he didn't wish to see her, or even speak with her, on her last evening at Hollridge, then she would not press him to.

Though, would he say goodbye to her when the time came?

"Tired already, Meg?"

Meg jumped, pushing herself away from the wall with a gasp.

She wielded her fan as if it were a saber until she realized whose voice spoke from the shadows.

She lowered her fan-turned-weapon and held it against her chest. "Matthew Pratt, you nearly scared me to death!"

He emerged from the darkness farther down the corridor, a grin lighting his face. "My apologies. I thought you knew I'd be in here."

Meg *should've* expected him. This corridor had always been their hiding place when Matthew had needed an escape from a ball or party. Now it was Meg who had needed the escape.

His soft footsteps slowly approached, bringing her mind back to the present. She wondered how he was still speaking with her, what with his avoidance of her these two days past.

Instead of asking the question that could potentially send him fleeing once more, she settled with another. "Have you been in here for long?"

"Only a moment or two."

"And who are you hiding from this evening, your mother or Society as a whole?"

A humored smile spread on his lips. "A bit of both. I didn't wish to partake in the game this evening. Especially as Sir Harry Hoax."

Meg could understand that. He was the worst sort of character to be, deceiving women into marrying him. Even as a game, it could lead to real heartache.

"Are you not worried your mother will find you and scold you again?"

He raised a single brow. "Do you not recall our bargain? You agreed to take responsibility when next we hid away. And I'm sure I don't need to remind you that I have already satisfied my end of the deal."

Heat rushed to her cheeks. How could she forget? That kiss had been in her memory and dreams ever since it had occurred, despite her attempts to forget it.

Matthew took a step toward her before she could respond, and she gripped her fan. "I came in here for another reason, as well," he said, his deep voice soft and slow.

"Oh?" Something in his expression unnerved her. Was it his

confidence? His unwavering stare? Whatever it was made her legs shake like a layered Christmas trifle.

"Yes. I came in here hoping to find you, to speak with you."

Meg bit her tongue, but she couldn't keep the question inside her any longer. "You do not wish to avoid me anymore then?"

Instead of any awkwardness or embarrassment she'd expected, Matthew stared at her with a stalwart expression. "No. I do not."

He spoke so resolutely, appeared so confident and without mirth, Meg couldn't help but stare. What was going on with him? Where were his skirting glances and nervous fidgeting?

"Well, I am here now," she said, crossing her arm over her stomach, his confidence seeming to sap her own. She ignored his dimples, his ruffled hair, and loosened cravat. Noting such things would only make her love him more. "So what do you wish to speak with me about?"

He moved closer to her, reaching out to take her hand in both of his. She could hardly draw in a single breath. "I wish to say a great many things. To explain. To let you know…"

He paused. Stroking her glove with his thumb, he stared into her eyes, and Meg's heart jumped. Was this truly happening? Was he about to say…

He continued, a half-smile on his lips. "I wish to let you know how I—"

"Sir Harry Hoax, is that you?"

Meg tore her hand from Matthew's and took a step away. Matthew remained where he stood, though his eyes focused on the entryway of the corridor to where a woman stood before them.

The light silhouetted her figure, hiding her face, but Meg would recognize that high-pitched tone anywhere. "Miss Josephine."

"I believe you mean Gipsy Caraboo," the girl corrected, taking a few steps forward. Her face became visible as she neared them, and she glanced between Matthew and Meg with a sly smile. "Why, Kitty Coy, I did not expect to see you back here. And with Sir Harry, of all gentlemen." She tapped his shoulder with her fan. "You, sir, are terribly naughty to bring such a timid creature as Miss Coy into the darkness to have your wicked way with her."

The girl was clearly still in character, no doubt enjoying herself to the fullest. If Sir Harry Hoax was terrible, Gipsy Caraboo was his equally horrible counterpart.

Knowing such, Meg should've disregarded her words, chalked them up to the game she played, but then…was Matthew playing that same game? Did that not explain his confidence, his sudden willingness to be near Meg?

She tried to dig out her worry, but a seed of doubt planted in her heart, and the roots began to spread deep as Miss Josephine continued.

"I know how you fear gentlemen, Miss Coy, but not to worry. I am here to save you from this man's clutches." She stepped closer to Matthew. "Now, Sir Harry, as the Gipsy Caraboo, I shall play your little game and take the place of Kitty Coy here."

Matthew took a step back, but Meg hardly noticed, still attempting to decipher the truth from the game. Matthew had said her name earlier. He'd admitted disliking his character. He wouldn't play a game and risk the chance of hurting her. Would he?

She glanced up at him, anxious to see his reaction to Miss Josephine's behavior, but when she saw a smile slowly spread on his lips, her chest tightened.

He wrapped his arm around Meg's shoulders and pulled her close to his side, facing Miss Josephine. Any other time, his proximity would have caused her to melt in a happy puddle on the floor. Now, she hardened, colder than the swirling wind outside.

"My apologies, Gipsy Caraboo," he said, "but I wish to be with Kitty Coy instead."

Perhaps if Meg had been of sound mind, she could have taken his words better. Perhaps if Matthew had not avoided her, had not shown her time and time again that he did not love her, she could have handled the ache piercing her heart. But hearing her character's name on his lips, instead of her own name, unraveled the hope binding her heart together, causing the pieces to slowly fall to the floor.

Tears sprung to her eyes, and she pulled away from his embrace. "I cannot do this," she said, backing away, ignoring his look of concern. "I cannot play these games any longer. Goodbye, Matthew."

"No, Meg, I wasn't…"

But she didn't listen to him. She darted past a stunned Miss Josephine and entered the ballroom, weaving her way through the dancers, praying to remain hidden as she fled from Matthew and the lie that he was not playing a game.

For she knew that he was.

CHAPTER 11

$\mathcal{M}$atthew stared at the entryway Meg had just darted through, cursing under his breath. Curse these games, these bargains. Curse his blasted stupidity. He'd only said her character's name to get rid of Miss Josephine, but it had clearly backfired.

He charged toward the entryway, making to follow after her, but Miss Josephine's touch on his arm made him pause.

"Excuse me," he said, pulling his arm away.

"What on earth is going on between you two?" she asked, her eyes wide.

He shook his head, inching toward the entryway. "It is nothing that should concern you, Miss Josephine. Please, excuse me."

"Oh, but Sir Harry, I am the Gipsy, remember?" She smiled coyly. "And I do believe you and Miss Coy must pay a forfeit now with your little mistakes."

Matthew's cheeks puffed out as he released a slow breath. He was a gentleman, and he needed to maintain his patience. But then, why did good manners matter when he needed to speak with Meg?

"Forgive me, Miss Josephine," he said, speaking each word clearly, "but I am no longer playing this game, nor shall I be paying any forfeits. You would do better to set your eyes on another gentleman tonight. Good evening."

Her mouth dropped open indignantly, and a small line wrinkled her brow. "Well, I never…"

He left before he could hear the rest of her complaint. As he entered the ballroom, he paused long enough to swing his head from side to side in search of Meg, but she was nowhere in sight.

Was she hiding amidst the guests, or had she already gone to her room? Either way, she clearly did not wish to be found, but he couldn't let another moment pass by without her knowing the truth.

He darted through the crowds, avoiding eye contact with those curious glances in his direction. He spotted the Bakers drinking away their sherry and port, laughing with the other guests, entirely unaware of the turmoil they'd created in their daughter's life. If Meg did not accept Matthew's declaration of love and still chose to go with her parents, he would never forgive himself.

He continued his search, moving from the ballroom to the card room. There was still no sign of Meg and her red dress, but when his eyes fell on his sister seated at a card table playing whist, he marched straight up to her.

"Louisa, I must speak with you for a moment."

Her smile faded away, and she glanced to the other three around the table, one of whom was Mr. Abbott. "Can't it wait, Matthew? We are in the midst of a game, as I'm sure you can see."

She widened her eyes in a warning to leave her be, but Matthew could not. He needed her help. Lowering his voice, he tipped his head to the side of the room. "Please, Louisa. Just a moment. It is urgent."

She frowned before nodding, turning to the other players, her eyes lingering on Mr. Abbott. "Please, excuse me for a moment. You may find another partner if you wish."

"I wish for no other partner but you," came his return.

Matthew stared at the man's blatant flirting that was clearly not character-driven, but as Louisa stood from her seat and crossed the room, he pushed the gentleman from his mind and focused on the task at hand.

He joined Louisa at the far side of the room, the two of them speaking low enough so they might not be overheard.

"Well?" Louisa asked, her hands on her hips, a look of flippant disregard on her face.

"Have you seen Meg?"

She raised her chin. "Yes. We have just spoken only a moment ago."

He stared at her expectantly, but she said nothing further. "And?"

"And, what? You expect me to tell you where she has gone after what you have just done to her?" She looked around the room, leaning toward her brother with a pointed finger and a scowl he'd never seen so fierce. "How could you, Matthew? You know how she feels about you. How could you pretend to fall in love with her for the sake of a little game?"

Matthew shook his head, his brow furrowed. "No, Louisa, I…" He trailed off in a growl of frustration. How had it turned into this? He lowered his voice, desperate to have the truth be known. "I was not playing a game. I was sincere. I was trying to tell her how I feel."

Louisa narrowed her eyes. "You mean…"

"Yes. I was trying to tell her how I…how I love her."

Saying the words aloud solidified his feelings, increased his desire to tell Meg tenfold, but as Louisa squealed, he pressed a hand against her lips.

"Hush!" He pulled his hand back and gave a short nod toward those in the room who watched them with apprehension.

"Oh, you stupid man!" Louisa said, wrapping her arms around him. "How wonderful this news is!"

He returned her embrace. "Yes, I think so, as well. Though I could do without the insult."

She pulled back, her hands on his shoulders. "Well, you are, aren't you? As foolish as ever a man was."

"I suppose I am. But I am trying to remedy the fact. Please, tell me where Meg has gone."

Louisa nodded, taking on a serious expression. "Meg came to

me earlier, saying she was to retire for the evening. I believe she will be in her room."

"Excellent, thank you, sister." He placed a quick kiss to the back of her hand. "Now do rejoin Mr. Abbott and warn him not to stare at you or I shall have to have a word with him."

Louisa's cheeks brightened, and he grinned in her direction before quitting the room and striding down the corridor to the front hall. He tugged off his gloves as he climbed the stairs, halfway up before his mother's voice called to him from behind.

"Matthew? Have you no decorum?" she asked. "You have just disrupted my party, tore through the crowds, and hid away from the dancers. What in heaven's name are you doing now?"

"I'm going to speak with Meg," he said, still continuing up the stairs.

"Well you won't find her up there."

Matthew finally stopped, turning to look at her over his shoulder. "Why? Where is she?"

"In the study. I had a feeling you might wish to speak with her this evening."

He narrowed his eyes as a smile tugged at her lips. Did she know? "What of Miss Mosely?" he questioned, testing the extent of her knowledge. "Is that not the woman I am supposed to speak with this evening?"

"Really, son. You and I both know she is not the young woman you actually *want* to be with, don't we?"

Matthew straightened, taking a step down the stairs, his heart racing. "How did you know?"

She gave him a dubious look. "*Everyone* knew but you, Matthew."

He moved down the rest of the stairs. "The bargain, the list of nine women, pushing me to find a wife and help with Father here, it was all part of your plan wasn't it? To help me realize my feelings for Meg."

"Of course it was." Her face softened, and she pressed a hand to his cheek. "I love you, son. And I wish for your happiness more than anything. But sometimes, a Mother must push her child if he proves thicker than a stack of bricks."

He huffed out a laugh. "Between you and Louisa, my confidence has suffered much this evening."

She patted him softly before motioning toward the study. "Go. She's waiting for you."

He nodded, and when she left for the ballroom, he turned down the opposite corridor and headed toward the study. His courage threatened to fail him with each step he took, but he squared his shoulders and continued on.

It was time. Time to set aside the games and teasing. Time to embrace the change before him. And time to speak openly and honestly with the woman he loved.

How he prayed she would hear him out.

Meg removed her gloves, setting them on a nearby chair before stoking the small fire in the hearth, prodding forth the heat from the logs. It didn't do much for the chill in the room, but she wasn't very cold anyway. The cool study was actually a welcome relief from the sweltering heat of the ballroom.

She eyed the closed door, wondering again when Mrs. Pratt would return. The woman had caught her just before Meg would have retired, begging her to remain in the study and speak with her. Before a word could be said between either of them, however, she'd excused herself without a reason and bade Meg to wait, that she would return in just a moment.

Yet, more than five minutes had passed, and Meg was still alone. Perhaps she ought to slip away to her room now. Mrs. Pratt would no doubt be asking her to remain at Hollridge, but nothing she could say would convince Meg to stay. Not now. Not after Matthew's insensitive teasing.

Distracting herself from her painful thoughts, Meg moved her attention to the window, staring at the large snowflakes falling in the darkness. She hoped the snow would stop soon so as not to disrupt her travel plans in the morning. She didn't want to remain a single moment longer than necessary in Haxby. Would she could leave tonight, slip away without another word or look at Matthew.

That would make it easier, wouldn't it?

The handle behind her rustled, and she turned to face Mrs. Pratt entering the room. Only, it wasn't Mrs. Pratt. It was her son.

Meg blanched. Her neck stiffened and eyes grew wide.

"Meg," he began, closing the door behind him as he stepped farther into the room.

His voice, her name on his lips, threatened to undo her, but she would not allow it. Why was he here? Had Mrs. Pratt told him where she was, or had this been her plan all along, to force them to reconcile?

She scoffed at the trickery. Like mother, like son. "What are you doing here, Matthew?"

Her voice was hard. Matthew stopped his advancement toward her, standing midway between her and the door. "You must allow me to speak with you, Meg."

The words triggered something within her, releasing hold of her senses and allowing anger to prevail. It was the same reaction she'd had when Matthew had prevented her from conversing with Mr. Kempthorne. Of course, she'd been grateful then to have a way out of speaking with the vicar, but it was not up to Matthew for him to decide with whom she spoke. Nor was it in his control if she listened to him or not.

"Oh, *must* I?" she questioned, shaking her head in disbelief. "*Must* I allow you to speak?"

He hesitated, seeming to rethink his words before he nodded. "Yes, you must."

"And why is that?"

His voice softened. "Because you misunderstood me earlier."

A ray of hope split through the darkness in her soul, but she ignored it, allowing her indignation to boil over. "I have misunderstood nothing, Matthew. You have made your feelings perfectly clear. From pursuing nearly a dozen women in a fortnight, to calling me your sister a number of times, to teasing me just now as that awful Sir Harry Hoax. I know you do not love me." Her voice broke, and she swiped away her hot tears. "And I will accept that. But do not tell me that I have misunderstood your feelings when you have revealed them to me so clearly."

She drew in a shaking breath, turning her back on him to face the window, unable to meet his eyes. She knew she shouldn't be so upset at him, but her anger was merely guarding her vulnerability, for she had expressed her love and received nothing in return.

His footsteps echoed around the silent room as he approached her from behind. "Meg, please, listen."

His gentle voice drew fresh tears to her eyes, and she nodded, slowly turning to face him, though her eyes remained on the small, orange flames in the hearth.

"I am sorry to have hurt you the way I have," he said. "But I hope I may make it up to you by saying now, with utter confidence that you are, indeed, mistaken in every way you have just mentioned in regard to my feelings for you."

Slowly, Meg raised her eyes to meet his. He stared at her without a hint of mirth, only certainty in his hazel eyes, and hope proliferated once more within her. She struggled to maintain hold of it, frowning as she shook her head. "That can't be true. The women you have seen this Christmastide—"

"Were sent directly to me from my mother." He reached into his jacket pocket, pulling out a scrap of paper. "You recall finding me in the front hall after we gathered the greenery from the house? This was the note I was reading." He extended it toward her. "I hope this will help you understand a little better."

Meg reached forward, retrieving the scrap of paper with two fingers like she would a soiled handkerchief. She didn't wish to look inside the note, having no idea what was written within, but at Matthew's encouraging nod, she slowly unfolded it.

What she found only confused her further—a list of nine women with her name at the top.

"What is this?"

"At the masquerade, once you left me alone with my parents, my mother struck a bargain with me, a bargain that was to be kept between myself and her. She promised to no longer interfere with my life choices if I agreed to get to know nine women from Christmas to Twelfth Night. Those are the nine women."

Meg could hardly believe his words. She knew Matthew was prone to accept wagers, and with such an outcome, it was little wonder he accepted it. But then…"Why is my name on the list?"

She glanced up at him, the corner of his lips raised. "My mother had her reasons."

Meg failed to find humor in the situation. If this list was based on women Matthew could marry, it hardly mattered that she was the first numbered. It only meant that she was part of his task. "So that's all this has been to you, that's why you have spent time with me, because of this…this game?"

He took a step toward her, a frown creasing his brow. "No, that is precisely what it has *not* been. I assure you, I have had a miserable time getting through this list. I have wanted to give up countless times, but the end goal kept me pushing through."

She scoffed. "So would you like me to congratulate you on your success? For working through your misery in meeting with me and eight other innocent women?"

Matthew's lips parted, staring at her senselessly before running his fingers through his hair. "No, you…" He trailed off with an aggravated sigh. "I am not accustomed to sharing my feelings, Meg, without teasing involved. You know this. I'm hardly making sense to myself."

The anger seeped from her heart, deflating her stamina and ending her will to continue the conversation. With sunken shoulders, she raised her hands in a shrug. "If you do not know your own feelings, Matthew, then how do you expect to share them with me?" She walked past him, pressing the list against his chest until he retrieved it. "This list ought to help you console you when I leave tomorrow."

She tried to move past him, but Matthew reached out his arm to stop her. "No, wait." He crumpled the paper in a ball and tossed it into the fire.

Meg watched it disappear into the flames before looking back up at him. He stared down at her. "Can you not see my feelings for you now, Meg? Can you not guess how I feel about you?" He gripped onto both sides of her arms, leaning down as he spoke clearly. "The past two weeks have been a torment, not because of the women I was forced to meet with, but because I could not spend time with the one woman I wished to…you."

Meg struggled to keep her head up, so intently did he stare at her. "I have never regretted accepting a bargain so deeply in my entire life," he said. "Even when you dared me to taunt those two hounds in return for a cake and we ended up running back to the house."

A smile tugged at her lips at the memory before he continued.

"I wasted away my time with my family. It put me in a despicable mood. And worst of all, it pulled me away from you. And yet, now…I see the wisdom of such a list. For not only did it force me to adapt and change—something you know I resist at every turn. But it also allowed me to finally see what everyone else already knew, including my parents, Louisa, and you."

He slid his fingers down her arms, moving to hold her hands. His touch sent pleasant tingles across her skin, sailing toward the warmth in her heart.

"I was finally able to realize that my feelings for you extend far more than sisterly love, far more than friendship. I finally realized that I love you. You, Meg Baker."

Her mind whirled. She could hardly believe his words. Could it be true? Could Matthew love her? A tear escaped her eye, trailing down her cheek, and Matthew wiped away the moisture, his hand lingering, cupping her face as he peered down at her. Her happiness radiated from her, her heart burning so brightly she feared it might burst forth.

"I was so afraid to change my life," he said, "to change our relationship. But now, I *wish* for it to change. I long for it to change. I want something more than friendship between us, Meg. I want you by my side, always. As my number one, my friend. My wife."

Meg would have thought she was living through some beautiful dream, but she knew the words coming from Matthew's mouth were far too wonderful for her own mind to conjure.

"Be my wife, Meg?" he breathed, leaning closer toward her. "Be my wife and remain with me forever?"

With a steady breath, Meg nodded. "Yes, Matthew. I will marry you."

His eyes lingered on hers, tears tinting the hazel to appear greener. He smiled, his lip pursed in a near tremble before he leaned forward and pressed his mouth on hers.

This kiss was different than the first. His lips were gentle, though they held a certainty to them. His hands moved to rest on her hips, holding her firmly in place with a sure grip as he tipped his head slightly to one side, deepening their kiss. Gone was her fear that Matthew would never return her love. Gone was her worry that she would end up without him. Instead, a sense of peace and joy filled her soul. A feeling of security she had never before known wrapped her in its embrace.

And finally, she felt as if she could breathe.

As Meg's hands slipped around Matthew's neck, pulling him closer to her, he knew without a doubt in his mind that declaring his love for her, creating a new life for the both of them, was the best decision, the best change, he had ever made.

He encircled his arms around her waist, pulling her against him. This was what had been missing from his life, and he hadn't even realized it. This was what he'd been longing for—love, security, hope for the future. How grateful he was that he'd found it with his friend.

Their lips moved in unison, their breath mingling and hearts pounding. Meg slid an arm down from around his neck, moving to rest against his chest until their kiss slowed.

As their lips parted, he rested his forehead against hers. "May I ask, when did your feelings for me change?"

Meg nodded against his brow, and he pulled back to peruse her face as she replied. "Last October, when you left for university. I knew I loved you, as I had never felt such a deep ache in my heart as when I watched you ride away."

He pulled back with a frown.

"Not the answer you were expecting?" she asked.

"Oh, no, it is not that. I merely forgot that I will be starting the new term next week. There is really no reason for me to attend, now that Mother will stop pestering me to marry and help here at Hollridge."

Meg reached up, running her fingers through his hair, sending his mind spinning. "I've had to wait months for you to love me. You can wait a few months for me to marry you."

They shared a smile before Matthew sighed. "Well, dear Meg. I do wish this moment could remain between just the two of us, but I fear we must include the others."

She pulled a face. "You mean, you wish to invite the eight women on your list to join us in here?"

He kissed the tip of her nose. "Heavens, no. Although they may be better behaved than the 'others' I am referring to."

She regarded him curiously before he called out toward the door. "You may come in now!"

The door flew open, and Matthew's parents and sister—Meg's new parents and sister—burst into the room.

"Oh, Meg!" Mrs. Pratt squealed, scurrying toward her with open arms. "How pleased we are to welcome you into our home as a permanent member!" She wrapped Meg in a warm embrace before pulling back, a look of sorrow sinking her features. "Can you ever forgive me for putting you through what I have these last two weeks? Surely you see I had to create that ridiculous list to get through my son's absurdly thick head and help him realize his love for you."

"Thank you, Mother," Matthew murmured, and Meg laughed.

"There is nothing to forgive, Mrs. Pratt," she said. "I only hope you are not disappointed in his choice of wife from your list."

"Oh, my dear. I put you on the top of that list for good reason." She winked. "All the rest were simply placeholders."

After another embrace, she stepped aside, allowing Louisa to hug Meg next.

"Now we shall be sisters at last," Meg whispered in her ear.

Louisa pulled back, shaking her head. "We have always been sisters, Meg."

Tears pricked Meg's eyes before Mr. Pratt reached for her hand, placing a soft kiss to the back of her fingers. "You have always been the perfect match for our son. How pleased I am that you have managed to convince him to change." He looked next to Matthew. "Although, I do believe you have some explaining to do, son."

Matthew chuckled, moving to stand beside Meg and placing his arm around her back. "Yes, I must apologize, Father. I shall not be able to accept that horse from you after all. Though, I'm more than happy to make the sacrifice."

He smiled at Meg, but all eyes turned to him in confusion.

Mrs. Pratt looked between her son and husband. "Horse? What horse?"

"Father promised me a new steed if I did not fall in love with any of the women you'd chosen for me," Matthew explained.

"Oh, did he now?" Mrs. Pratt asked, turning a raised brow on her husband. "You were intentionally trying to sabotage my plan, Mr. Pratt?"

Mr. Pratt raised his hands. "I was merely having a bit of fun watching him squirm. I knew Matthew would be unable to deny his love for Meg for long." He winked, turning to Matthew. "But the horse is still yours, son. Consider it a wedding gift."

"Truly?" Matthew looked down at Meg. "Oh, you must see him, Meg. He's beautiful. I'll let you ride him first if you wish."

As Meg smiled up at Matthew, Mr. Pratt held out his arm to his wife. "Shall we return to the party?"

Mrs. Pratt slid her hand around her husband's arm. "Oh, yes.

They will be wondering where we have gone. And Mr. Abbott will no doubt be wishing for Louisa to return, as well."

Meg met Louisa's gaze with a knowing look of her own.

Her friend merely giggled behind her hand before darting from the room, her parents following soon after.

"I suppose we'd better join them," Meg said. "I must find my parents and inform them they shall have to find another way to become family with the Malcolms."

Matthew took her hand and placed it around his arm. "Does that upset you?"

"Not in the slightest. You know there is nowhere else I would rather be than here at Hollridge, with you."

Their eyes met, and mutual feelings of love and adoration passed between them before they made their way from the study and toward their bright future ahead.

EPILOGUE

Yorkshire, Christmas Day

"Are you not ready yet?"

Meg glanced to the door as her lady's maid departed and Matthew entered her room, an impish grin deepening his dimples. He closed the door behind him and crossed the room toward her.

"You know I like to take my time, Matthew," Meg said, eying her reflection in the mirror. "Besides, I wish to make a good impression for Christmas dinner."

He bent down, pressing a kiss to the side of her neck. She shivered with delight.

"No one is here but the six of us this year," he mumbled against her skin. "Who are you trying to impress?"

She stood to face him, and he straightened with a teasing smile.

"My husband, you nonsensical man," she responded.

He pulled her against him, his hands resting at the small of her back. "You always make an impression on me, my dear. Even when you look like a tree."

He motioned to the berries she'd had her lady's maid place in her hair again for Christmas this year, and she swatted his chest before pulling at his lapels and bringing him down for a sound kiss on his lips.

As he pulled away, he looked down at his jacket. "Now look what you've done. My cravat is all amiss and my jacket is near-wrinkled."

She shook her head with an airy sigh. "They were like that before, Matthew, as per usual."

He winked, and Meg smiled up at him, pressing a hand to her stomach. "Are we ready to share our news with the others this evening?"

His eyes sparkled. "Indeed. I have been dying keeping this to ourselves for so long."

"Matthew, it's hardly been a month."

"Well I know that. But I—"

His words were interrupted by a large pounding on the door, followed by heavy footsteps and giggling trailing down the corridor.

"Blast them both," Matthew growled, darting to the door. Meg laughed as he poked his head out into the corridor. "They're nowhere in sight."

"There is always tomorrow to beat them, I suppose," Meg suggested.

She smiled, thinking of Louisa and Mr. John Abbott, the squirrel. They had come to stay at Hollridge for Christmastide and had made it a habit to pound on Meg's and Matthew's doors each time they went downstairs, goading that they were made ready before either of them. How terribly wrong Meg had been about the man. What she'd thought to be dullness had merely been his shyness.

After Matthew had returned from his final term at Oxford, he and Meg, and Louisa and Mr. Abbott, had been married in a double ceremony. Mr. Abbott had taken a few months to become comfortable around the Pratts, but once he was, he had proven to be an even worse tease than Matthew himself.

"Come along," Matthew said. "If we wait too long, John will be plotting to beat me at another horse race with Father again."

Meg smiled. "Yes, just a moment." She pulled open the drawer of her writing table and retrieved a few peppermint drops, popping one into her mouth before extending the other to Matthew.

"You and your peppermints," Matthew said with amusement.

"What? It is the one sweet I cannot live without during Christmas."

"Is that so?" Matthew asked, pulling her into his arms once more. "Well you are the one sweet I cannot live without ever."

Meg pulled a face.

"Too much?" he asked.

She laughed. "No, I loved it. Almost as much as I love you."

He reached down, placing a kiss on her brow. "Oh, dear Meg. What would I ever do without you?"

She sniffed. "No doubt end up alone with a stable full of horses."

"Now that doesn't sound all that bad."

She swatted his arm, and he chuckled. "But I must say, I far prefer a life with you."

And as he bent down, placing a lingering kiss on her lips, she couldn't help but think the same about Matthew, her best friend, her love, the father of her future child, and her very own number one.

THE END

Read the next book in the series by Kasey Stockton, "A Duke for Lady Eve"

Purchase Deborah's next Christmas book, "On the Second Day of Christmas"

Purchase the next books in the new series: The Belles of Christmas – Frost Fair

Belles of Christmas

Book 1 - Unmasking Lady Caroline by Mindy Burbidge Strunk
Book 2 - Goodwill for the Gentleman by Martha Keyes
Book 3 - The Earl's Mistletoe Match by Ashtyn Newbold
Book 4 - Nine Ladies Dancing by Deborah M. Hathaway
Book 5 - A Duke for Lady Eve by Kasey Stockton

Belles of Christmas - Frost Fair

Book 1 – Her Silent Knight by Ashtyn Newbold
Book 2 – All is Mary and Bright by Kasey Stockton
Book 3 – Thawing the Viscount's Heart by Mindy Burbidge Strunk
Book 4 – On the Second Day of Christmas by Deborah M. Hathaway
Book 5 – The Christmas Foundling by Martha Keyes

These books may be read in any order.

AUTHOR'S NOTE

The games played throughout this story actually appeared during the Regency Era, including short answers, whist, loo, and hazard. The game of characters, enjoyed during the Twelfth Night revels, was also playing during the Regency period, but for the sake of this story, I used them a little earlier than when they were actually around. (See "Winter Evening Pastimes; Or, a Merry-Maker's Companion" by Rachel Revel (pseud.) for more fun games played during the period!)

One more note, did you happen to catch each of the items from the song, "The Twelve Days of Christmas"? They're not in any specific order, but throughout this story, I have each item mentioned, some more subtle, while others more obvious. I couldn't very well write a book titled "Nine Ladies Dancing" and not include the song in some way!

If you enjoyed "Nine Ladies Dancing," please consider leaving a review. And if you'd like to receive the latest news about my future novels, sign up for my newsletter. I always share newly released and discounted clean romance novels, as well as fun polls, quotes, and giveaways. My newsletter subscribers are also the first to see sneak peeks and cover reveals!

Make sure to follow me on Facebook (for more clean romance deals) and Instagram (for photos of my travels to the UK and more).

I hope to connect with you soon!

Deborah

ACKNOWLEDGMENTS

I don't think I've ever had as hard a time writing a book as when I wrote "Nine Ladies Dancing." Perhaps it was because I was trying to channel my inner love for Christmas during the blazing, boiling months of July and August. I had to use my imagination more than ever to picture cold snow falling from the blue skies or sitting before a fireplace instead of my air conditioner. That being said, it is now extremely satisfying to have this book in the hands of you, my wonderful readers. Such a feeling of satisfaction couldn't be possible, however, without the help of so many of my friends and family!

First, to the other authors in the "Belles of Christmas" series: Mindy Burbidge Strunk, Martha Keyes, Ashtyn Newbold, and Kasey Stockton. I loved getting to know each of you better. Thank you for the laughs, the fun, the commiseration, and the help!

Thank you to my editor. Yet again, you have saved another one of my stories from being utter garbage. The time you put into each of my books and the advice and encouragement you share is simply perfect. Thank you!

To my critique partner, fellow author, and wonderful friend, Arlem Hawks. What would I do without you? From helping me fix those first plot holes to ensuring this story was better line by line, I owe so much of my progress in this book—and as a writer—to you. I will be forever grateful for the blessing you are in my life!

Last, I need to express my gratitude to my sweet husband. Christian, how you put up with my craziness, I'll never know. What I *do* know, however, is that I would be nothing of what I am today without you. Your support, your help, your patience, and your excitement for my stories is incomparable. *Thank you.*

ABOUT THE AUTHOR

Deborah M. Hathaway graduated from Utah State University with a BA in Creative Writing. As a young girl, she devoured Jane Austen's novels while watching and re-watching every adaptation of Pride & Prejudice she could, entirely captured by all things Regency and romance.

Throughout her early life, she wrote many short stories, poems, and essays, but it was not until after her marriage that she was finally able to complete her first romance novel, attributing the completion to her courtship with, and love of, her charming, English husband. Deborah finds her inspiration for her novels in her everyday experiences with her husband and children and during her travels to the United Kingdom, where she draws on the beauty of the country in such places as Ireland, Yorkshire, and her beloved Cornwall.

Made in the USA
Coppell, TX
25 March 2022

75474388R00098